GIANT

of the

VALLEY

ALSO BY HARRY GROOME

Wing Walking

Thirty Below

The Girl Who Fished with a Worm

The Best of Families

Celebrity Cast

Giant of the Valley

and

The Witness

NOVELLAS

HARRY GROOME

THE
CONNELLY
PRESS

Library of Congress Control Number: 2019916694

Cover design by Delaney-Designs

Composed by Terry Bradshaw, Stamford, NY

The Connelly Press, Villanova, PA

ISBN: 978-1-7341309-0-4

for Lyn

Giant of the Valley

'Tis the infirmity of his age:
yet he hath ever but slenderly known himself.
—*King Lear*

PROLOGUE

L ouis McCutchen, "Big Louis" to most everyone outside his family, said he remembered that early December evening in 1993 like it happened yesterday, even though, as you'll soon see, remembering yesterday isn't exactly what you'd call Big Louis' strong suit. He remembered placing his hands on the white linen tablecloth as he prepared to leave his club, only then asking his wife if she'd like a cappuccino. Katherine had declined, saying that they really should get going, that the weatherman was calling for eight to ten inches before the storm moved off the coast. He remembered helping Katherine with her long down coat and pulling her navy cashmere scarf snugly at her throat and, as always, marveling at her beauty and how much he loved her.

With the snow blowing into their faces, Big Louis took Katherine's arm, and they walked slowly to their car, testing their footing every step of the way. After ushering her into the passenger's seat and scraping the windows free of snow, once seated in the frigid Taurus, he turned the heater on high, fastened his seat belt, and looked at the love of his life. "Would you buckle up just tonight? Please. For me?"

Katherine smiled and patted the sleeve of his heavy Loden coat. "If, and when, it becomes the law. You know it makes me feel claustrophobic. Besides, you can't teach an old dog new tricks."

"Oh, but you can, you know, with patience and reward."

"Who would know better than you? But it's okay, Louis dear, with you at the helm, we'll be fine."

"You're sure?"

Katherine said she was sure.

Big Louis drove slowly, checking his brakes every few hundred yards to test the road conditions. "Must be two inches already," he said. "You'd think the salt trucks and the plows would have been out long ago."

"But isn't the first snow always so beautiful?" Katherine asked. "It seems to quiet everything, and I love the way the flakes appear and then disappear in the headlights, almost as if it was their destiny."

As he turned onto the crest of the hill on their familiar route toward home, the taillights of the cars ahead of him began to glow on and off in rapid succession. Big Louis took his foot from the accelerator, but his car failed to slow. Gripping the steering wheel tightly, he cursed. "Must be a patch of ice." The cars down the hill slid from one lane to another, one spinning 180 degrees and plowing into a large elm on the side of the road. Big Louis tapped his brakes to see how the Taurus would respond. The car's rear end fishtailed and closed on the cluster of cars no more than thirty yards ahead. "Your seat belt, Katherine," he bellowed. "Please, fasten your seat belt!"

Katherine struggled to find the seat belt buckle without taking her eyes off the chaotic scene ahead. Big Louis' heart was pounding and he stepped down on the brake pedal as hard as he could, knowing his wheels were sure to lock but hoping that somehow it would slow his car. At first, the Taurus slid sideways and then seemed to pick up speed, whiplashing in a dizzying circle, wrenching the seat belt buckle from Katherine's hand as she fumbled with locking it in place.

Big Louis said he will be haunted forever by the thunderous thud that followed and the sound of breaking glass as his car spun head-on into a panel truck, his seat belt unyielding as the Taurus caromed into a second car before jolting to a stop. "God damn it," he said and looked at Katherine, curled on the floor beneath the dash, her forehead and much of her blonde hair glistening with blood.

He asked if she was all right. When she didn't answer, he asked if she could hear him. He hurriedly unlocked his seat belt and reached for her to lift her back onto her seat. "Please, be all right," he said. "For God's sake, Katherine, be all right." He brushed nuggets of glass from her hair and her coat and tried to inch her from beneath the dash when he heard a loud tapping sound. He turned to face a woman bundled up against the storm holding a small dog on a leash. She was frantically signaling that she wanted to talk with him. Big Louis lowered his window, and the woman pushed back the hood of her parka and peered into the car and laid a gloved hand on his shoulder. "Whatever you do, please don't move your passenger. An ambulance should be here any minute. They'll know what to do."

"But, it's my wife," Big Louis said. "She's unconscious."

"So, I see," the woman said and asked if Big Louis was injured. He repeated that it was Katherine who was hurt. The woman nodded and told him that she was a nurse, that she would see if there was anything she could do when flashing lights and barking sirens cut through the quiet of the falling snow as an ambulance and two police cruisers sped toward the mangled cars. Big

Louis reached for Katherine and patted her still form. "I'll be right here. We're getting help."

The nurse turned back to Big Louis and pulled his door open. He stared blankly at her, confused by the sound of vehicle doors slamming and the staccato noise of a police radio. She asked if he needed help and took his arm to steady him as he emerged from the car. "Careful," she said, "it's really slippery," and asked for his name.

"It's not me; it's Katherine who's hurt. I have to get her home."

"I understand, sir, but, first, what's your name?"

Big Louis shook his head as though he disapproved of the question, like it was an invasion of his privacy. "McCutchen. Louis McCutchen."

"All right, Mr. McCutchen, please try to remain calm while the EMTs free your wife from the car."

Big Louis remembered grabbing the woman by the shoulders and holding her to look into her eyes, searching for the truth, and asked, "Is Katherine going to be okay?"

A little after one in the morning, a doctor appeared in the patient waiting area at Massachusetts General Hospital and asked if he could have a word with Mr. McCutchen. All the color drained from Big Louis' face as he hurried to join the doctor. He had already begun to pound his fists into his thighs in anticipation of the news he was about to receive.

Katherine's death was the reason Big Louis said to hell with Boston and all its fancy doctors, the doctors who couldn't save the only woman he'd ever loved; her death the reason he said to hell with the Gillette Company where he was no more than an irregular heartbeat from becoming the company's next CEO; her death the reason he bundled up his girls and his bird dogs and moved—lock, stock, and barrel—to a remote valley in New York's Adirondack mountains, far away from the place where everywhere he turned he was reminded that he had walked away from the crash with barely a scratch while Katherine had absorbed its full force.

The pain of not having her by his side, wondering why he hadn't been more assertive and demanded that she wear her seat belt was too damn much, but in the tiny, close-knit hamlet of Levi Lamb, he slowly found the peace and healing that he was searching for.

At least until recently, when his story began anew.

ONE

For the many years since the accident, Sunday lunch with one of his daughters was one of the few things that Big Louis looked forward to. One warm June Sunday, it was Eleanor's turn, not only to cook her father his mid-day meal but to provide him with some companionship other than his Llewellin setters and, frankly, to check in to see if Big Louis was holding his own or losing ground.

With patches of snow still showing on the summits of Mount Marcy and Whiteface, Eleanor hiked the steep two miles up Bobcat Mountain. She carried all she needed for lunch in an Adirondack pack basket and arrived at the foot of her father's dirt drive on the dot of noon, a fact that pleased her because promptness was the way Big Louis liked things: familiar, predictable, precise. Now more than ever, following routines was not only important to him but important to her, and her sisters as well, because unexpected events seemed to both confuse their father more than they once had and agitate the living hell out of him, something for which his daughters usually paid a hefty price.

Eleanor paused, hunched her wicker pack into a more comfortable position, and wondered why her father's aging bothered her more than it did Julia and Robin. Lost in this puzzling thought, she followed the path to the house, stopping by the lean-to where Big Louis still spent many a night. The smell of the balsam boughs woven to create the lean-to's flooring reminded her of the nights she and her older sisters had slept there the first summer after their mother died. She was twelve and thought her oldest sister Robin, her colorful, sexy idol, had abandoned her by going to Georgetown rather than a nearby college. But in the lean-to, their sleeping bags in a tidy row like cordwood, she'd never felt as loved, as much a part of her family, or as safe as she had then and there.

As she approached the kennels, the Llewellins stood on their hind legs, wagged their black and white tails, and pawed at the gate. She greeted them by name—Sweetheart, the old lady; Tray, the stylish hunter who was coming into his prime at the age of four; and Blanche, the irrepressible puppy—and stuck an index finger through the wire mesh and tickled each on the nose. She was about to head to the house when her father called to her: "Let those trundle tails out if you would."

Big Louis greeted her at the front door. As always, he was clean-shaven, for shaving every day, like everything else under Big Louis' sun, was part of what he called his "belief system;" the system that began when he was a trainee at the Gillette Company, with its Blue Blades that made you "look sharp, feel sharp, and be on the ball, every time you shaved." But, like so many things with Big Louis, there was more to it than met the eye. To him being unshaven made old men—especially those whose beard and hair had turned snow-white like his—look like derelicts. Even worse, it made them look like they'd given up, "like they no longer gave a rat's ass about playing the game of life."

With a hug and a kiss, he said, "To what do I owe this honor?"

Eleanor took his hand and turned him to face her. "Sunday lunch, Dad. Your favorite: Vichyssoise and hamburgers."

"Of course. Of course. Sunday lunch." He squeezed her shoulders and kissed her again. "Well, don't just stand there. Come on in. You know where the kitchen is."

Eleanor couldn't tell if this was a question disguised as a statement but let it pass with a smile. In the well-stocked kitchen—she and her sisters and Big Louis' property manager, Owen Strait, made sure he always had everything he needed and wanted—Eleanor laid out the contents of her pack on the kitchen island and opened the refrigerator to retrieve the mayonnaise and ketchup. (Hellmann's and Heinz, of course. Big Louis felt that stocking only the leading brands at the Hodgepodge, his brainchild that started as a small grocery store with a New York-style deli section and morphed into the unofficial center of the community, cut down on the number of choices his customers had to make, and Big Louis believed that the one thing people secretly hated to do was make decisions.) To her surprise, Eleanor found his house keys, car keys, and the keys to the Hodgepodge sitting in a pile in front of an empty milk carton. She turned to say something, but her father had gone outside to comb the setters. She watched through the kitchen's bay window and thought he was still an imposing and impressive figure, his hair a luxurious white in the noonday sun, his large hands expertly grooming the dogs while he smiled and talked gently to them. Her pale blue eyes—a gift from her father—began to tear as she thought, *It's not fair. Just not fair.* She put the empty milk carton in the trash and hung the keys in their customary place on the hook by the kitchen door, then wiped at her tears with a dish towel and muttered, "Enough of that. Let the games begin."

At lunch, Big Louis asked how Eleanor's painting was going. *A good start*, she thought and said that she'd been quite productive lately and pleased with much of her work but couldn't reach agreement with her gallery on the timing of her next show.

"Those prima donnas who run those galleries in Boston sure are a precious bunch," Big Louis said.

Eleanor reminded him that her gallery was in New York.

He raised an eyebrow. "Since when?"

"Since always." She thought that her frustration with her father's confusion and failing memory was evident in her reply and softened her tone. "Almost since the day I graduated from RISD."

"RISD?"

"The Rhode Island School of Design, Dad. You should know; you wrote the tuition checks."

"Why, of course. RISD," her father said and laughed. "It's not easy keeping up with the three of you."

"I have a bit of trouble at times, too." She smiled and asked if he'd like some coffee. When he declined, she said, "That's a first," but Big Louis shrugged as though he hadn't heard her. She fussed with her knife and fork, neatly arranging them on her plate in the manner that her father prescribed, and took a deep breath. "Dad, I think we should talk."

"About what? The Sox? Not much to talk about there."

"No, Dad, for once not about baseball; about—"

He interrupted her. "Oh, let me guess. Good news. You've got a boyfriend."

Eleanor shook her head and looked down at her plate. "No, Dad. No such luck." She thought, *no such luck for him but not for me*, and wondered when the time would finally be right to tell him about April, her long-distance partner in Saranac Lake.

"Whatever happened to all those guys who used to hang around the house?" Big Louis asked.

Eleanor said none of them were quite right for her.

"Well, you've always had high standards. That's one of the things that makes you so special, but you're not getting any younger, you know. Your mother had all three of you well before your age."

"No one knows that better than me." She forced a smile and tried to collect her composure. "But not getting any younger is what I wanted to talk to *you* about. I'd like to discuss your plans for your future; how you're going to make the best of the time you've got left."

"Time I've got left?" Big Louis laughed. "You know something I don't? Like I'm about to croak?"

"That's the whole point: nobody knows what the future will bring. My guess is that you've got plenty of good years left, so the question is, how are you going to spend them? And where and with whom?"

Big Louis pushed his chair back as though he was anxious to end the conversation and leave the table. "I plan to keep on doing what I've always done, right here with you and your sisters and the Llewellins. What's wrong with that?"

"There's no right or wrong, Dad. It's just that I think you should consider spending more time in a community of friends. You know, to keep you stimulated and have them with you if you ever need help."

"Help? What the hell are you talking about?"

"As a precaution. Just in case something bad happens. That's all. I mean, what would you do if you slipped in the shower and broke your hip or something, and you were all alone?"

"First of all, that isn't going to happen," he said. "And second, if it did, I'd call one of you or Owen."

"I guess, but you'd be better off if you had someone right there to help you. And Robin and Julia and I would feel better about it too."

"And where would all this wonderful stuff happen?"

Eleanor hesitated and wondered why she was the one who always ended up delivering the hard news to her father. Finally, she said, "The Cliffs."

Big Louis shook his head in an animated fashion. "The Cliffs? That goddamned place? No way. That place is for people who can't remember their own names or wipe their own asses."

Eleanor had known it was coming but flinched all the same. "But Dad, the DeForests and the Cliffords and lots of your other friends are already there or have put their names on the list. Will you at least think about it? Give it some serious thought? That's all I'm asking."

Big Louis mumbled something under his breath and then asked, "Did your sisters put you up to this?"

Eleanor said no, no one had put her up to it.

"So, it's just you who's turning on me? You should be ashamed of yourself. You're the last one I thought would do that."

"Dad, please. I'm not turning on you. It's simply a fact of life that as we age, we change and must accept it and learn how to deal with it."

"Well, mind your own business, and look after yourself and find yourself a husband, for God's sake. I don't need your help, and if I go anywhere, I'll live with Robin or Julia. That's the least they can do for me."

Eleanor reached for her father's hand to calm him. He started to pull away but then covered her hand with his. The look in his eyes seemed vacant. She waited for him to say something more, but he sat in silence, his lips trembling. Finally, she tried to push away the hurt of his comment about finding a husband and said, "Dad, believe me, I'm not turning on you. That's the last thing in the world I'd ever do. I'm just worried that as you get older silly little things like going up and down stairs or driving at night will become harder and harder. At The Cliffs you wouldn't have to worry about stuff like that, and we wouldn't have to worry either."

Her father patted her hand. "There's no need for you to worry. I'm doing fine, just fine."

They sat without speaking for a moment before Big Louis asked if Eleanor was going to offer him coffee, reminding her that she always did.

TWO

Ravi Rajapakse was stretched out on his leather Barcalounger recliner, sipping his morning coffee and studying the financial reports in *The Wall Street Journal*. Except for a Rockwell Kent watercolor of the great range, he was surrounded in his spacious Timberpeg post and beam cabin by lots of things some folks might call "rustic," but many would call "Ticky-Tacky Adirondacky."

On the more traditional, rustic side of the ledger, a black bear rug lay yawning in front of the walk-in stone fireplace; a forlorn-looking moose's heavily-antlered head drooped above the birch bark mantle, and the chandelier over the dining room table was fashioned from intertwined white-tailed deer antlers.

On the more controversial side, a highly varnished 15-foot Adirondack guide boat was suspended from the living room ceiling, and a mounted coyote lay underneath the front hall table, looking up at all who passed it by.

Ravi wore an outdated Yankees' World Champions 2009 cap with rose-tinted Maui Jims perched on top of it. Copies of *The*

Economist, *Barron's*, and *Adirondack Life* were stacked on the floor within his reach. He was engrossed in a report of an IPO for a company with the nonsensical name of Alibaba when Julia burst into the living room, waving her hands about her head as though she was being chased by a swarm of bees. "First, it's rattlesnakes, and now it's deer ticks. Next, it'll be the crocodiles."

Ravi checked his watch and noted where he'd finished reading in anticipation of what might become a drawn-out discussion. "Crocodiles? In Essex County? Really?"

"That's what that professor from Princeton said would happen if we don't do something about global warming."

"I think he said that over time we could have *alligators* in the Adirondacks, not crocodiles."

Julia set Ravi's *Wall Street Journal* on the floor and curled her willowy figure in his lap. "For the umpteenth time, Ravi, if you enjoy correcting people so much, why don't you get a job at the correctional institute up in Ray Brook?"

And Ravi said, for the umpteenth time, that he was just trying to be precise and factually accurate; that it was an old habit from his days on Wall Street.

"Well, who cares what they're called, Lord of the Facts. They're enormous, scary things that could eat one of our kids if we don't do something about them."

"Hypothetically correct. Alligators can devour small children and dogs." Ravi hesitated. "But let's go back to the timber rattlers."

"Ravi, bag the stupid snakes," Julia said. "Right now, the issue's deer ticks and Lyme disease. And I'm not kidding."

"Surprising new data."

"Well, there you have today's surprise, my love, so what do we do?"

"Get to the root of the problem."

"The ticks?" Julia asked.

"No, the hosts. The deer," Ravi said.

"But Dr. Winston says that field mice are as big a problem as the deer."

"Are you sure about that, or are we talking crocodiles versus alligators here?"

Julia climbed from Ravi's lap and looked down at him. "I don't care how many gazillions you made at Lehman, Ravi; you should never have retired. What is it that they say; an idle brain is the devil's workshop?"

Ravi crossed his legs and studied his highly-polished tasseled loafers. "I think it's *idle hands* that are the devil's workshop. It's an idle *brain* that's the devil's playground."

"Please, please, please, Ravi, you're like a dog with a bone. Let's drop the crocodiles and the alligators, okay? And the rattlesnakes and the brains and the playgrounds. The issue is Lyme disease and our kids' health. And maybe yours and mine, too."

"You've got a point, but we'll never be able to get rid of the mice."

"No, but we could get rid of the deer."

"How?" Ravi asked. "Get a SWAT team in here to eradicate them? They'd just come back—"

"Uh-uh, Ravi, they can't come back if we build a fence to keep them out."

"And piss a lot of people off in the bargain."

"Like who?"

"Like your dad and your realtor-sister, for starters, plus a whole lot of folks in the homeowner's association and the High Peaks conservation group."

"Well, if so, so be it. What is it you always tell me? The only thing in life that's constant is change? Well, it's about time all of them joined the twenty-first century and accepted the new reality. So, call Spence's Fences, and let's get cracking."

She slung her leather backpack over her shoulder and jingled the keys to her SUV, the only Mercedes within miles of Levi Lamb with an Obama YES WE CAN. AGAIN. bumper sticker, and said that she was off to Burlington for a routine checkup and couldn't miss the ferry.

Ravi asked if she'd like some company.

"You're sweet, but you should be here when the kids get back from camp." She giggled. "You know, before we're overrun by alligators."

"You're sure?" Ravi asked again.

"I'm positive." She blew him a kiss goodbye. "Love you."

"And me you," Ravi said. "A whole lot."

THREE

The more Eleanor thought about her lunch with her father, the more she was a whole bunch of things: worried, hurt, and disappointed, but mostly she wished she'd pursued the conversation about The Cliffs more effectively. While her father's memory loss and confusion seemed a little more pronounced than in the past, it was his living by himself at seventy-eight that upset her the most, and she wished she'd sold the concept of not living alone more convincingly, although, to what end, she had no idea. But, she'd planted the seed if only her father could remember what she'd said.

She debated which of her sisters to call first. She flushed when she considered flipping a coin, chalking it up to "baby sister syndrome," and dialed Julia, the softer, more understanding of the two. Almost before Eleanor could get out her greeting, Julia said, "Sorry I've taken so long to check in with you, but recently I've been dealing with the mysteries of medical science. So, how was lunch?"

"Not a barrel of laughs," Eleanor said. "Far from it. But tell me, are you okay?"

"I think so. It's not the most elegant of topics, but I've got God awful hemorrhoids." Julia paused as though she might say more, then said, "Enough of that. How was Dad? Bad, horrible, none of the above?"

"Mostly worrisome," Eleanor said. "Forget the fact that he keeps his keys in the fridge and thinks my gallery's in Boston and can't remember whether or not I've offered him coffee. It's just so damn obvious he shouldn't be by himself. He's not only forgetful; he's confused and less and less the loving man we all used to worship. And, I think down deep he's aware of his problem and it scares him. Believe it or not, it scared me enough that I bit the bullet and suggested that he consider The Cliffs."

"The Cliffs? Really? Wow, Ellie, as always, you've got more guts than I have."

"Fewer brains may be more like it."

"I'm guessing that The Cliffs didn't go down all that well?"

"That's the understatement of the year. He thinks places like The Cliffs are for old people, not people like him."

"Ah, yes, the indestructible Big Louis McCutchen."

"The one and only," Eleanor said. "And he thinks I've turned on him."

"Just because you were trying to help?"

Eleanor began to cry. "It kills me to see that great man, the guy the three of us relied on for everything, absolutely everything, becoming so sealed off, so unsure of himself and becoming angry about it. It's horrible and frightening, but not just for him, but for me, too."

Julia said maybe he should take a memory pill or something, that she'd talk to Sandy Janeway about it on her next visit.

"He's already taking pills for his blood pressure and his cholesterol—if he remembers to take them. But yes, maybe a new pill. No matter what, he shouldn't be living alone, and it would be great if you said something to him and if Robin would, too. And maybe Owen; Dad might listen to him. But be prepared. He says if he needs to go live somewhere, he'll move in with Robin or you."

"That'll be the day."

Eleanor said she understood and would call Robin to bring her up to date. Before hanging up, she asked, "Are you okay, really? And Ravi? And the kids?"

"Right now, there's nothing else to report," Julia said. "The little ones are fine, and so is Ravi, although he dearly needs something to do. The good news is he's just volunteered to be in charge of building a fence around our property, something that should keep him occupied for a while."

"A fence around your property?" Eleanor said. "Your entire property?"

"The whole enchilada," Julia said. "A deer fence to prevent deer ticks. You know, to make us safe from Lyme disease."

Eleanor hesitated. "Does your easement allow that?"

Julia said that wasn't an issue.

Eleanor asked if she'd checked her documents.

"No need," Julia said. "Ravi and I don't have an easement."

"You've got to be kidding," Eleanor said. "Wasn't our deal with Dad that we'd put conservation easements on our properties once we owned them to protect them from development in the future?"

"Right, but Robin says it's not a smart business move, and she should know."

"Robin doesn't have one either?"

"Robin doesn't have one either."

"Well, live and learn and shame on you both," Eleanor said. "Does Dad know?"

"Of course not, silly. All that would do is upset the apple cart."

"What about Owen?'

Julia said maybe Owen knows, but maybe he doesn't.

"And you and Robin don't plan on telling them?"

"Not unless they ask."

"So, I'm the only one who has eased her property?"

"Looks that way," Julia said.

"Oh, boy," Eleanor said. "You better hope Dad doesn't find out. It would devastate him."

"Not much chance of that. I mean, who would be nasty enough to tell him?"

As soon as Eleanor ended her call with Julia, she dialed Robin. The phone rang and rang and rang before her sister picked up and greeted her with, "Hey, Babycakes! How're things?"

"Pretty good. And you?"

"Close to perfect. Coming up on forty and still kicking ass. I'm working on a humongous commission up on Upper St. Regis, one that I just might steal right out from under Sotheby's nose. How's that for an ice-breaker?"

"Sounds good for you, but I'd like to talk about Dad and . . ." she hesitated. "And some other stuff."

"It's your nickel. How was Sunday, the fun day?"

Eleanor said that their father's dementia seemed to be getting worse, that his situation was worrisome enough for her to suggest that he move to The Cliffs.

"Babycakes, you are a wonder. Stuff like that is usually left for the oldest sister, not the youngest."

"That's one of the reasons I'm calling the oldest sister."

Robin laughed. "Time for me to hang up."

"Don't you dare," Eleanor said. "All I'm asking is that you support me on this, that we present a united front."

"Glad to. I'll pay Dad a call this week."

"That would be great, but be forewarned. He says if it ever gets to the point where he has to move somewhere, he'll move in with either you or Julia."

"That'll be the day."

"That's exactly what Julia said. She also shared some other interesting tidbits, like she's worried about Lyme disease, and she and Ravi are building a fence around their property to keep the deer out."

Robin laughed again. "Not going to happen as long as I chair the Homeowners' Association. Besides, tell me what's wrong with this picture: An immigrant comes to our country with our open borders, gets an Ivy League education, makes God-only-knows how many million on Wall Street, retires at the ripe old age of thirty-four, and then builds a fence around his palace to keep others out."

"But it's not for people," Eleanor said. "Just the deer."

"It'll work for both," Robin said.

Eleanor didn't know what to say and didn't want to start an argument, especially one that would lead nowhere. Finally, she said, "Let's leave Ravi out of this for a moment and talk about the fence."

"What's there to talk about?" Robin asked. "It's a fucking deer fence; maybe the only one in the Adirondack Park, by the way. It'll be eight feet high and will lower the value of the adjacent properties. That includes your studio plus all the others I've been trying to sell for the last few years. I'm sure that Dad and others at the High Peaks Conservation Trust will shit a brick, but I'll find a way for the LLHA to stop it."

"Because it'll be an eyesore or because it'll violate Julia's easement?"

"Because it's guaranteed to be ugly as sin and will upset the natural . . ." Robin hesitated. "Whoa! Hold the phone. Julia has eased her property?"

"No," Eleanor said. "You told her not to."

"No, no, no, Babycakes. I didn't *tell* her not to. I just told her that it wasn't a good business decision and would cut off too many options."

"Even though Dad gave us our properties with the understanding that all of us would place conservation easements on them?"

"Not legally enforceable," Robin said. "We never signed an agreement."

"And Dad thinks I'm the one who's turned on him?" Eleanor said. "Wow, wouldn't he be surprised?"

"He sure would be, but he won't be," Robin said, "because, as of now, it's our dirty little secret."

"Maybe Julia's and yours, but not mine."

"Sorry to say, but it's yours, too, Babycakes. You know, 'Unus pro omnibus, omnes pro uno,' and all that good shit."

Eleanor asked her what the heck she was talking about.

"One for all and all for one. The Three Musketeers' motto. And it's our motto starting today, so you'd better get used to it."

"Now we're the Three Musketeers?" Eleanor said. "Isn't that kind of silly?"

"Works for me," Robin said. "At lots of levels."

For a moment, neither spoke. Then Robin said, "Good talk, Babycakes. Gotta run. Big, big hugs."

Eleanor asked if she'd promise to talk with their father.

"I promise," Robin said, "if you promise, you won't."

FOUR

Robin and Big Louis were perched on the deacon's seat of his lean-to, drinking Saranac Summer Ale and basking in the late-day sunshine. Robin raised her beer toward her father. "Here's looking at you, Dad."

Big Louis tapped his bottle against hers. "To you. And, as always, to Katherine."

"And as always, to Mom," Robin said.

For a moment, neither spoke. Finally, Big Louis said, "God, but I love the view of the great range from here. Never want to leave it. Funny, I even find the howling of the coyotes comforting, like they're trying to tell me they're my new neighbors."

"That's a doozy," Robin said but quickly added, "The view centers me, too, Dad. That's one of the reasons why I'm here."

Big Louis asked if she wanted to talk about a Homeowners' Association issue.

"Kind of. Kind of business but kind of family, too. Kind of a mess, frankly."

Her father said he knew she'd fix whatever the problem was. "That's one of your many strengths. You've always been an excellent problem solver."

"Maybe not this time," Robin said. "And I may need your help. It has to do with Julia and Ravi. They're planning on building an eight-foot-high fence to keep out the deer—"

"That ought to do the trick," Big Louis interrupted.

"—around their entire property. I think it's a horrible idea, and I'm guessing that my board will be one-hundred percent against it. I think it'll tighten a lot of sphincters of your Conservation Trust members, too."

Big Louis laughed. "Well, it'll give us something to talk about other than all those damn invasive species coming in from China."

Robin shook her head and turned toward her father to say that it wasn't a joke, that it was a real dilemma, stopping short of saying it was a fucking disaster.

Big Louis continued to smile. "Don't worry, your sister and Ravi can't do it. Their easement doesn't permit it."

Robin was surprised that her father had zeroed in on the heart of the matter so quickly. While he was known for his laser-like analysis in the past, not so much in recent years. She thought maybe he wasn't as far gone as Eleanor had said but took him by the arm to make sure she had his attention. "Dad, Julia and Ravi don't have an easement."

"But wasn't that part of our deal?" Before Robin could answer, Big Louis said, "I'll double check with Owen."

Robin said there was no need to bother Owen; Ravi and Julia never eased their property.

"Well, goddamn it, if that's the case, leave it up to me. Maybe I'll change my mind about the gift to them. In the McCutchen family, a deal's a deal; no ifs, ands, or buts about it." He sat for a moment nervously wringing his hands and then said, "God, I love the view of the great range from here. It's home to me. Without your mother, it's all I've got left."

Robin nodded. "But what if someday you can't continue here by yourself?"

Her father looked at her as though he was puzzled by her question. "Well, fall's right around the corner. I'll be hunting grouse in a couple of months. Just like always."

"But what would you do if you got tangled up in some blowdown and broke your leg?"

"What the hell do you mean, what would I do?" He chuckled. "I'd get my leg fixed. That's what I'd do."

Robin set her beer bottle between her feet and rested her head in her hands. "I'd hope you'd get it fixed, Dad. That's not the issue, and, again, it's not a joke. The issue is: what if there wasn't anyone around to help you? Or what if you took a header going down stairs? Or God only knows what else. What then?"

"Well, it ain't going to happen." He slapped his thighs with open hands, pushed himself to his feet, and struggled to gain his balance.

Robin reached for his hand to steady him. "We're not through here, Dad, so please, sit down."

Big Louis sat like an obedient child. "What now?"

"Dad, I'm asking if, at your age, you think it's okay to be living alone?"

"Why the hell not? I'm doing fine. Although I miss..." He paused.

"I know, we all miss Mom, but if you had more friends around you, maybe her loss wouldn't hurt so much."

"What the hell do you think I should do? Move in with you?"

"Even better, Dad, why don't you move into The Cliffs with people your age, where everything is pretty much taken care of for you?"

"With a bunch of morons who can't remember their names or wipe their asses? Good lord, who have you been talking to?"

Robin admitted that she'd had a chat with Eleanor and that they both thought that he should consider it.

"That Eleanor," Big Louis said. "How come she doesn't have a boyfriend? What in Sam Hill is wrong with her?"

"Nothing, Dad. Absolutely nothing," Robin said.

"You sure?"

"I'm sure. Ellie's fine."

Big Louis said he wasn't so sure. "And what about Julia? Is she turning on me, too? Are you all forgetting everything I've done for you?"

"No one's turning on you, Dad. Just the opposite. We're trying to figure out what's best for you."

"My willful daughters," he said. "Two down, one to go, and nobody on base."

Robin muttered, "Oh, for Christ's sake," and asked him to please consider The Cliffs, that it would be great if he did.

"And what would I do with the dogs?" He shook his head. "No, I'm fine right here. Just fine." He finished his beer and tapped the mouth of the bottle with his index finger. "Are the rugrats enjoying Groton?"

"I wish you'd stop calling them rugrats," Robin said. "They're teenagers now and—"

"What? Rugrats not politically correct enough for you? I would think paying their tuitions gives me some liberties."

"Of course, and Henry and I thank you every day for what you do. It's just—"

"Just nothing. Absolutely nothing. If it's anything, it's that the three of you have gotten so goddamned complicated; have so many new-fangled ideas and issues, that it's . . . it's almost unnatural." He paused for a moment but continued to tap the mouth of his bottle. "Groton was so great when I was there."

"For sure," Robin said. "Louis and Hobey love it, too. Believe it or not, Little Louis isn't so little anymore; next week, he starts looking at colleges."

"I guess I'm on the hook for that, too."

"I thought that was the plan."

"We'll see," Big Louis said. "We'll see. If you all can change your minds and not do what we agreed to, well, I can, too."

Robin started to say something more but thought better of it and wrapped her arm around her father's waist. "Henry and I love you and appreciate what you do for us so very much. Please, never, ever forget that."

Big Louis nodded and shaded his eyes from the sun that hovered above the mountains. "Never want to leave this place," he said. "Never."

Robin said she'd received the message. Loud and clear.

FIVE

Big Louis and his property manager, Owen Strait, had gathered for their daily get-together. With three Llewellin setters, Owen and Big Louis' 6'5", 260 pounds in place, plus stacks of back copies of *Field & Stream*, *Outdoor Life*, and *Sports Afield* strewed across the floor, the small office in the Hodgepodge felt lived in, if nothing else. Before getting down to business, Big Louis ordered the setters on their beds. The routine of settling the dogs followed the same order it had the day before and the day before that, for Big Louis believed that dogs and people were most comfortable with the predictability of routine.

First to be told "down" was Sweetheart, whose arthritic hindquarters made it difficult for her to get up once she'd lain down and whose eyes were clouding over with cataracts. Next was Tray, Big Louis' prized hunter, whose alert brown eyes accented his spotted white and tan muzzle and black forehead and ears. And, finally, the ten-month-old Blanche, who tried to climb into her master's lap before he set her on her bed and told her in no uncertain terms to "stay."

Big Louis began the morning's routine by asking Owen what the hell was going on with his daughters, Julia, in particular. (Hard to believe, but Owen was considered an outsider, "from away," as the locals like to say, even though he grew up in North Elba less than fourteen miles to the west of Levi Lamb. What's more, his wife Donna, who was born "to hell and gone" in Saranac Lake, was viewed as an interloper too, although she and Owen had lived in the valley for close to twenty years.)

Owen held his coffee at arm's length and stepped carefully over Sweetheart, who was sleeping spread-eagle on her back, half-on, half-off her bed. Once seated in his usual chair, he said, "All set. What's the issue?"

"That's what I just asked you," Big Louis said.

"About what?"

"What the hell is this, Owen, a 'who's on first' routine?" Big Louis ran a hand over his face as though he was checking his morning shave. "By the way, what's happened to our closer? He sure did stink the place up last night."

Owen had hoped that for once, just once, he might get away without discussing the last-place Red Sox and tried for quick closure. "One game a season doesn't make."

"Who said that?" Big Louis asked. "Shakespeare?"

"Don't think so, but it's true, and Uehara will be fine. Now, back to your question."

Big Louis hesitated and then said, "Oh, yes," like he'd just remembered why they were meeting. "I'd like to review what we decided with the girls about their easements. I need a little refresher."

"Right," Owen said. "A little refresher." He moved to Big Louis' desk, where he unrolled a Map of Survey that showed all of the McCutchen landholdings. "Here, take a look."

Big Louis stood, placed his large hands on either side of the map, and bent forward to study it. "How many acres are we talking about?"

"Not including your parcel?"

"Of course, not including my parcel," Big Louis snapped back. "My IQ's not set at room temperature, you know."

"No one's ever accused you of having a low IQ," Owen said and smiled to reassure his boss that he was on the right track. "We're talking about seventy-five acres, neatly divisible by three."

Big Louis stared at the map without speaking.

After an awkward moment of silence, Owen reached across the map and circled each highlighted subdivision with his index finger. "Lot A was for the Honeywells; B for Julia and Ravi, and C went to Eleanor. Each has a stretch of Nye Brook and great views of the mountains. All have good access. It's exactly the way you wanted things: fair and square, and with the girls treated like adults."

Big Louis laid a hand on each subdivision as though he was giving it his blessing. "It was supposed to do away with any squabbles after I kick the bucket. Right?"

"Right. That's what you wanted, and that's what they agreed. What's more, this way, they got a tax deduction, not you, and you wanted to give them that as an incentive to put conservation easements on their properties."

"Sounds like a damn good plan. So, what the hell is going on?"

Owen said that Robin and Julia hadn't eased their properties.

"Isn't that a breach of contract or something?"

"I'm afraid not. You never signed a formal agreement."

"Well, answer me this: can I change my mind and renege on the gifts?"

Owen sighed. "Again, I'm afraid not. They took title to their properties over three years ago."

"And I'm just finding out all of this now?" Big Louis shook his head. "Why didn't you tell me?"

"I thought it was a family issue between you and your daughters. I didn't think it was my place to get involved."

Big Louis returned to his chair and picked up the *New York Times* from the floor. "I don't know about you, Owen. I just don't know."

Owen shrugged and dismissed Big Louis' comment; he'd heard ones like it many times before and asked Big Louis if he wanted him to talk to his daughters.

"No. I'll handle them myself," Big Louis said.

"Let me know if you change your mind," Owen said. "Now, if you've got the time, I do have one other item."

"Which is?"

"Making Henry the manager of the Hodgepodge."

Big Louis stared at Owen for a moment as if this was a new thought for him. Finally, he asked, "You think it's a good idea, or don't you want to get involved with that either?"

"Come on, Louis, that's not fair," Owen said. "Of course, I want to get involved. This is about the future of the Hodgepodge, not about tattling on your girls. What's more, it's with you in mind. You've created the center for the community with this store. And, having founded the Conservation Trust, you're viewed as one of the driving forces in conserving the Adirondacks. What more can you ask? Now's the time to let go of the reins, to spend more time with your grandkids and your dogs. You've earned it, and I think you owe it to yourself."

"But what if Henry screws it up?" Big Louis said.

Owen asked what made him think his son-in-law might screw it up.

"I don't know. There are times I wish Robin had married a . . .

a guy who went to one of the Ivies . . . a more experienced and sophisticated businessman."

"Give him a chance," Owen said. "He's a real hard worker, and he's great with your customers. With your coaching, I think you can make him a success."

"But what if he spends more time fishing than he does running the store? Then what?"

"Then, you take the job away from him."

"That simple?"

"That simple," Owen said. "Don't forget, you'll always be the owner, the ultimate boss."

Big Louis smiled at the thought of being the boss, the way he used to be back in Boston. He asked Owen to give Henry the news of his promotion before the week was out. He opened the *Times* to the sports section. "For four million dollars shouldn't the Sox be guaranteed a win every time Uehara steps on the mound? I don't get it, Owen. I just don't get it."

SIX

Robin surveyed the people sitting around Sandy Janeway's dining room table and tapped her coffee cup with her folded glasses, calling the meeting of the Levi Lamb Homeowners Association Board of Directors to order.

While only 68 of the 193 homeowners were members, the LLHA was by far the most influential entity in the hamlet. It was the tail that wagged the dog and, if you happened to be lucky enough to be elected as one of its seven directors, you had a lot of sway over almost everything that went on in the valley. But, the fact that the LLHA was chaired by one of Big Louis' daughters, and the local realtor, to boot, stirred up a lot of pretty nasty comments about Robin's conflicts of interests and, on at least one occasion, her other extracurricular activities.

Once all were settled, Robin leaned toward a small black speaker in the middle of the table and asked, "Father, can you hear me?"

From the other end of the line, the Reverend Stuart Quinlan said he could hear her "like a voice from heaven."

"Peachy," Robin said. "Along with you, Father, we've got Sandy, Owen, Peter Trout, and Eleanor. Minnie Savage sends her apologies. She's on a yoga retreat in Nepal." Robin struggled unsuccessfully to keep a straight face. "Developing her inner peace or something like that." She checked the notepad in front of her. "So, if it's okay with all of you, I think we can assume that, as per usual, sister Eleanor's minutes of our previous meeting are dead solid perfect, and we can get on with why I called this meeting."

All nodded in agreement. Their discussion is best summarized in Eleanor's minutes that followed:

```
Chairperson Honeywell opened the September
    9th, 2015, meeting with the following state-
    ment: "The issue we're faced with this morn-
    ing is the proposed eight-foot-high deer
    fence that would surround the Ravi and Julia
    Rajapakses' entire twenty-five acres."
Question from Dr. Janeway: "What's the fence
    for?"
Chairperson Honeywell: "It's intended to
    keep out the deer, to protect their fam-
    ily from Lyme disease."
Considered medical opinion from Dr. Janeway:
    "A real health issue and one that is get-
    ting worse and must be addressed."
Question from Owen Strait: "Have the Ra-
    japakses submitted a plan to us for our
    review, or are we just discussing the con-
    cept in principle?"
Chairperson Honeywell: "The latter."
Question from Forest Ranger Trout: "Do we
```

have the authority to approve or disapprove?"

Secretary McCutchen: "There's nothing in the bylaws that addresses fencing of any kind."

Chairperson Honeywell: "Well, I guess we could always amend the bylaws."

Dr. Janeway: "Can we legally do that *post facto*?"

Chairperson Honeywell: "*Post facto*, Sandy? Really?"

Dr. Janeway: "After the fact."

Father Quinlan (via the phone): "I'm confused. What, exactly, is the issue?"

Chairperson Honeywell: "The fence would be an eyesore and would lower everyone's property values."

Forest Ranger Trout: "And it would degrade the forever wild nature of the hamlet."

Father Quinlan (via the phone): "We wouldn't want that."

Question from Dr. Janeway: "But there's nothing to prohibit it?"

Chairperson Honeywell: "Nothing but a reduction of property values, an affront to the natural world, our role as stewards of the community, and common sense."

Owen Strait: "Haven't you overlooked one other important consideration?"

Chairperson Honeywell: "And what would that be?"

Follow-up question from Owen Strait: "How does your father feel about all of this? Is this what he envisioned when he gave the parcels to each of you? Especially when he hoped that the three of you would place conservation easements on your land?"

Secretary McCutchen: "There's no easement being violated here."

Forest Ranger Trout: "Are you sure?"

Owen Strait: "Sure, she's sure, because there's no easement on the property."

Father Quinlan (via the phone): "So we don't have any authority to approve or disapprove. Is that right?"

Chairperson Honeywell: "Unfortunately, that's right."

Follow-up question from Father Quinlan (via the phone): "I'm a bit handicapped by not being there, but I sense the majority are against the fence?"

Chairperson Honeywell called for a vote. All present voted against the construction of the proposed eight-foot-high deer fence that would surround the Rajapakses' entire twenty-five acres except for Secretary Mc-Cutchen, who abstained.

Chairperson Honeywell informed Father Quinlan that the vote showed four against the fence with one abstention and asked how he voted.

Father Quinlan (via the phone): "I make five
    against. As such, madam chairperson, what
    do we do now?"
Owen Strait suggested the board send a let-
    ter to the Rajapakses outlining its con-
    cerns, asking them to reconsider building
    the fence and consider other options.
Chairperson Honeywell asked if all agreed.
All agreed.
Chairperson Honeywell adjourned the meeting
    at 11:12 am.

Eleanor's minutes didn't record that, off the record, Chairperson Honeywell volunteered that this topic was personally upsetting because it involved her sister and brother-in-law. The
minutes also didn't reflect that Robin was tempted to tell Sandy
Janeway that she knew what *post* fucking *facto* meant; and that
she was relieved to stay out of the middle of a family squabble and
was fucking delighted with the outcome of the meeting.

SEVEN

Julia and Robin held each other close for quite a while, perhaps to reassure each other they'd always be the best of friends no matter what was to follow. Before they separated, Julia said, "Many, many happy returns of the day."

Robin kissed Julia on the cheek and smiled. "Can you believe it? A fucking milestone, for sure, but many happy returns? You sound just like the old fart." She pointed to the lone chair in her small office. "To what do I owe this honor?"

Julia giggled. "Now, you're the one who sounds like Dad."

"Right, except he always says that because his brain is becoming tapioca pudding, and he relies on others to let him know what's going on. For me, it's nothing more than a straightforward question."

Julia raised an eyebrow. "Really? You're wondering why I'm here?"

Robin moved to her cluttered desk and switched off the ringer on her phone. "Yes, really."

Julia fished a piece of paper from her leather backpack and handed it to her sister. "You're honestly surprised that I might want to talk to you about this?"

Robin studied the letter she'd written as chairperson of the Levi Lamb Homeowners Association for a moment without speaking.

"Come on, Robin," Julia said, "you must have known this was going to upset me. Please, level with me."

Robin dropped the letter on her desk. "Okey-doke, on the level. Why didn't *you* level with me and tell me you were considering making your property a mini-Auschwitz before it became a public issue?"

"Oh, my heavens, Robin, what's gotten into you? Couldn't *you* have talked with *me* first? And I'm guessing you've already talked with Dad."

"You're not the only oyster in the stew, Julia, so before you go off halfcocked, think about it. I've got to answer to the Homeowners' Association's board on issues like this, plus I've got my customers, past and future, to think about. And, you're right, there's always Dad, although it would have been better if you'd stepped up and told him yourself."

"I'm sorry, Robin, I really am," Julia said. "I've been preoccupied with some other stuff, but none of that explains why you didn't talk with me first."

"Here's why: this is your fence, your fucking issue, not mine. So, own it. I'm just reacting to the problem you've created for the community. That's my job, and while it's up to you and Ravi to decide how you spend all of his Wall Street millions, it's up to me to bring some sanity to Levi Lamb's development."

"But the fence is to keep the deer out, so our kids don't get Lyme disease. What's wrong with that?"

"First, there's no guarantee, fence or no fence, that your kids won't get bitten by a tick. Second, it'll be a fucking eyesore."

"Wow, Robin, you've gotten so . . . so tough."

Robin stood over her, hands on hips. "Pragmatic is more like it. And, for people like you who live in a worry-free economic bubble, it may come as news to you that that's what it takes to survive in this dog-eat-dog world."

Julia swiveled in her chair to face her sister. "Come on, Robin, Ravi and I aren't the only ones who have few economic concerns. I mean, it's not as though your loving Honeybunch, Henry Cabot Honeywell, was brought into this world a pauper; born with a silver spoon in his mouth is more like it."

"But Henry rolls up his sleeves and goes to work every day like every other guy in the hamlet except your Ravi."

"Wow," Julia said, "I never knew you resented Ravi's success. A lesson learned, for sure." She shrugged. "But does all of this mean you have to use the f-word all the time?"

"Does it offend you with all your kumbaya double-talk?" Before Julia could answer, Robin said, "Reconsider the fence and try, for once, to imagine life outside your little bubble."

Julia stood and switched the keys to her SUV from hand to hand. She looked at Robin, her eyes filling with tears. "Good advice, I guess."

"What's up with you?" Robin asked. "Really."

Julia dismissed Robin with a wave of her hand. "Nothing. I'm just a scaredy-cat." She turned to leave, then stopped and forced a smile. "Love you."

"No fence, no foul," Robin said and blew her sister a kiss goodbye.

After Julia left, Robin stood by the bay window of her office, steadying her well-worn binoculars. "It couldn't be. Or could it?" She grabbed her reading glasses and referred to the *Sibley Guide to Birds* that was open in front of her. "Sweet Jesus, it is. It's a Bicknell's thrush! After all these years."

She continued to study the small, gray-brown thrush, occasionally referring to Spotted Thrushes in her *Sibley Guide* to make sure—*absolutely sure*—that she had identified the bird correctly when the thrush flitted into the thick cover of hemlocks and maples that framed her small lawn. She thrust both hands above her head and bellowed, "Jesus H. Christ! Number 600 on my life list, and it's a fucking Bicknell's thrush! Well, happy fortieth birthday, Robin, who's bob, bob, bobbin' along."

She collapsed in the chair at her desk and pulled her bird watcher's journal towards her. She tried to calm her shaking hands before recording her sighting of a Catharus bicknelli. Once finished, she hooked her glasses on the top button of her blouse and sat for a moment, staring vacantly at the void that the thrush had left in the branches of the hemlock where she had first seen it. *Some birthday. My boys packed off for Groton and my Honeybunch fishing for trophy brook trout in the wilds of Labrador, and now the Bicknell's disappeared, too.* Suddenly, she felt very much alone, dismissed, and taken for granted. Henry's obsession with fishing—"ripping lips," he called it—and managing the Hodgepodge had left time for little else, and that little else rarely included her. And, with both her sons off at boarding school, being an empty-nester made her feel that her life had very little, if any, purpose. And, to top it all off, she was at odds with one of her sisters over a fucking deer fence.

Her phone rang, and she debated whether she should answer it or let her answering machine handle the call. She would much rather talk to the local Audubon folks about her recent sighting, but she picked up the phone out of habit. "Black Fly Realty. Robin on the horn. How can I help?"

The caller was Frisky Forsythe, who said she'd seen a new listing on Rocky Peak Lane that sounded just adorable, just the right size for her, and wondered if she could sneak a peek.

Robin reached for her appointment book when she heard a knocking at the front door. She told Frisky she had a visitor and asked if she could hold for just a sec. She set the phone down and hurried to the door, stopping in the hallway to check herself in the mirror. *Not bad for forty. Not bad for thirty, either.* She forced a smile and wondered who she was kidding. She moistened her full lips and fluffed her brown curls that hid strands of white; unhooked her glasses from her blouse and unbuttoned another button—*no two more buttons*—and said, "Well, that should do it," and reached for the handle to the door.

A moment later, she picked up the phone and told Frisky she'd get back to her ASAP. "Someone's just delivered a birthday present, and I'd like to put it where I can enjoy it."

She started to hang up the phone but stopped. "All this for *that*, Jordan?" she said, and then, "Oh, sweet Jesus, Honeybunch, you weren't due home until tomorrow."

EIGHT

Big Louis and Owen had taken their customary, well-worn places, and the Llewellins were curled on their beds, but only after Blanche had, once again, tried to climb into her master's lap. To start Big Louis off on the right track, Owen gently reminded him what he wanted to discuss. "You wanted to talk about some family stuff?"

Big Louis fiddled with the leather lanyard with two Day-Glo orange whistles dangling at its ends that hung around his neck as though he hadn't heard or understood Owen's question.

Owen hesitated. "You said you wanted to talk about something Eleanor had said that upset you."

Big Louis shook his head. "It's not that important." He sipped his coffee. "You watch the boys last night?"

"Yeah. Any time we beat the Yankees—"

Big Louis interrupted him. "By the way, when in God's name are we going to get a TV cable in the hamlet? My satellite reception stinks."

"Agreed," Owen said. "Cable would be great, and you could throw in a cell tower, too. But let's get back to Eleanor."

"God damn it, Owen, didn't I make myself clear? It's not that important."

"You sure?" Owen asked when there was a knock on the door.

"Now what?" Big Louis said and called out, "Who's there?"

"Sorry to bother you, Mr. McCutchen," a man said from the other side of the door. "It's Peter Trout, and I'd like a minute of your time. We've got a bit of a situation."

Big Louis leaned toward Owen and lowered his voice. "Who is it?"

"Peter Trout. The Forest Ranger."

"What's he want?"

"It sounds like he has a problem and wants to talk to you. Give him a minute. He's a good guy."

Big Louis shrugged and signaled for Owen to open the door.

Forest Ranger Trout stood in the doorway, holding his stiff-brimmed Smokey Bear hat with both hands. He greeted Owen with a handshake, then said, "It's nice to see you again, Mr. McCutchen. How are you doing?"

A smile animated Big Louis' face as he registered that he knew the Ranger and, more importantly, that the Ranger knew him. "I'm fine, thanks. To what do I owe this honor?"

The Ranger remained in the doorway. "A hiker has gone missing. He was last seen up Bobcat near the brook yesterday, and we wanted to alert you that there will be a number of search parties in your area. Nothing to be alarmed about."

"Probably some greenhorn from New York or Montreal," Big Louis said. "We've got too goddamned many of them. The black flies aren't doing their job."

Ranger Trout laughed. "Not this time, Mr. McCutchen. He's from Connecticut and has been scouting the Adirondacks looking to buy some property. Nothing more than a heads-up, sir. But, if you would, please keep an eye out."

After the Ranger had said his goodbyes, Owen asked Big Louis if he wanted to continue their talk.

"Nope. All done for now. Maybe some other time. Right now, I think I'll give the Llewellins a little exercise." He struggled to stand, causing the setters to abandon their beds and turn in circles, wagging their tails. He smiled at them as he opened the door. "Maybe they'll even hunt up the hiker. Same time, same station, tomorrow?"

"Same time, same station, tomorrow," Owen said. "Maybe we can talk then?"

"Maybe," Big Louis said. "We'll see."

It's not uncommon for someone to report a missing hiker in the Adirondacks. With more than six million acres of trees, streams, and lakes and the peaks of 46 mountains defining its skyline, the Adirondack Park is not only the largest park, state or national, in the lower 48, it's a haven for hikers who want to come face-to-face with its beauty. As a result, close to 350 hikers go missing every year in the Park. Most have either gotten lost or broken a leg, while occasionally someone dies of a heart attack, and, from time to time, there's a hiking-related death, usually from a fall. And, once in a blue moon, someone disappears into the High Peaks to commit suicide.

The hiker Peter Trout reported to Big Louis was a man named Jordan Groves. He was forty-four and lived in Greenwich, Connecticut. Late Wednesday afternoon, his lawyer called 911, saying that Groves was missing. After the call, the State Police found his BMW 750 at the foot of the Clarence Petty trail. Groves hadn't made an entry in the trailhead register, and nothing was in his car other than his registration and insurance cards, real estate brochures from LandVest and Sotheby's, and an unopened box of Cohiba Esplendido cigars.

NINE

Henry Honeywell tapped lightly on Sandy Janeway's rough-hewn front door, almost as though he hoped the doctor wouldn't hear him. He waited a moment, debating whether he should knock again when a slight man with eyes and ears that made him look a lot like one of the bats that hang around almost everybody's basement in the Adirondacks opened the door.

Dr. Janeway took one look at Henry's face and said, "My Lord, good buddy, what in the world happened to you?"

Henry ignored the question and thanked the doctor for seeing him.

"Sure, sure. Any time," Dr. Janeway said. "Let me get a better look at you."

Henry followed him through the house to his office, where Dr. Janeway told him to sit and switched on an examining light above his chair. He studied Henry's bloody mouth and battered hand for a moment. "What happened?"

Henry looked away from the light and said he'd had an accident.

"No, shit, Dick Tracy," the doctor said. "And how, exactly, did this accident happen?"

Henry paused as though he was trying to remember. "I was going to rip some lips with a stonefly nymph over on the west branch." He paused again. "And I was walking down a steep bank near the Wilmington Notch and . . ." He paused a third time. "And I took a header. Took a goddamn header, Sandy. My wading shoe got caught under a root, and I did a face plant on a rock." He looked up to see if the doctor had gotten the picture.

Dr. Janeway laughed. "Ripping lips, redefined. You break your rod?"

At first, Henry looked puzzled by his question and then said, "Uh, no. That's the only good part of the story."

"Hard to believe," Dr. Janeway said.

Henry said it was God's honest truth.

"If you say so," Dr. Janeway said. "Now, let me take a closer look." As he began to clean away the caked blood on Henry's lip and hand, he asked what the water temperature was.

Henry shrugged. "Never got that far, but I'd guess the Ausable's in the mid-seventies right now."

"With the river like bathwater and not a cloud in the sky, and you went fishing for trout? Get real, Henry. What were you thinking?"

Henry sighed. "I needed to get out of the house."

"I get it, the old 'for better or for worse but not for lunch' syndrome." The doctor slid a tongue depressor in Henry's mouth and told him to say "ah," then threw the depressor in the trashcan and crossed his arms across his chest. "Your hand's pretty badly banged up, but I don't think you've broken any bones. It's a miracle you didn't break your rod. Your lip needs some stitches, and you've chipped a couple of teeth. I can fix your lip, but you should see the oral surgeon in Lake Placid about your teeth." He adjusted the light over Henry's chair. "Okay to stitch you up?"

Henry said, "Be my guest."

As Dr. Janeway wrapped a blood pressure cuff around Henry's arm, he said, "So if you don't mind me asking, what's going on that makes you want to escape from the home-front?"

Henry shook his head. "Hear no evil; speak no evil."

"Huh," the doctor said. "I thought that we agreed we'd always level with each other, you know, both personally and professionally." He squeezed the blood pressure bulb, watched the mercury go up and then down. When he was done, he hooked his stethoscope around his neck. "Your blood pressure's quite high. One-fifty over one-ten. When we're through here we'll talk about getting it under control."

"Not to worry, Sandy. I'm fine," Henry said. "It's just that I've got a lot going on right now."

"Still don't want to talk about it?"

Henry patted his friend's arm. "Nope, but don't take it personally."

"Okay. Okay. Now a little Lidocaine, a few small stitches, an antibiotic, and you'll be back ripping lips in no time." He raised the needle and tapped Henry's lip with his fingers. "A little pinch coming up."

While he waited for the Lidocaine to have its numbing effect, the doctor asked, "By the way, how's Julia doing?"

"She's fine. Flaky as ever, but just fine. Why do you ask?"

Dr. Janeway shrugged. "Just asking. As a friend."

Once home, Henry sat motionless in his Subaru, admiring his surroundings. The sky was a crystal-clear robin's egg blue, and an occasional orange or yellow leaf floated from the maples that bordered his drive, signaling that fall was on its way. He thought that he'd led an idyllic life if only . . . if only he hadn't caught his wife half-dressed on the floor of her office with some stranger.

He closed his bruised right hand into a fist as though he was going to punch someone, then rested it high on the steering wheel to study it. He shrugged. *No one will notice it in a few days.*

He ran a finger over the stitches in his lip and turned the rearview mirror to evaluate them. *Taking a face plant on the west branch is as good a story as any.* He looked in the mirror one last time and screamed, "Fuck! After all these years and she's cheating on me? Fuck me!"

He entered the house quietly and was greeted by Goldilocks, their Golden Retriever. He gave her ears the expected massaging and started toward the master bathroom to shower away the dirt, the blood, perhaps even the anger that clung to him, when Robin called from her office, "That you, Honeybunch? I've been worried sick."

Before he could answer, Robin appeared at the bathroom door, her eyes swollen and red. She took him by his shoulders and turned him toward her. "Oh, my God, look at you. Are you all right? I'm so sorry, Henry. So very, very sorry." She wrapped her arms around his waist, lay her head on his chest, and began to sob. "Oh my God, what have I done? What was I thinking? Please forgive me. Please, Honeybunch. Please?"

Henry wanted to push her away; wanted to tell her that they were finished, that he'd wasted nineteen years of his life being faithful to her. But all he could spit out was that he didn't know if he would ever be able to forgive her. He lifted her chin and forced her to look at him. "Why should I forgive you when there's no way to get even?"

Robin's eyes were awash with tears. "Because I love you but thought you no longer loved me."

"Bullshit," Henry said.

"No. Not bullshit. You're so wrapped up in all your own stuff and show so little interest in me, what else would I think? If it were you, what would you think? And then you weren't even going to be with me on my big birthday—"

"But I'd planned to surprise you all along—"

Robin laughed through her tears, "Well, you sure did that."

"I'm surprised it hasn't happened before," Henry said.

"You shouldn't be. There haven't been any 'befores.' Besides, nothing really happened." She sniffled and wiped at her tears. "And he did that to you?"

Henry nodded. "I chased him up toward Adrian's Abyss but lost him in the woods."

"So, this whole thing's our dirty little secret?"

"It had better be, for your sake."

"And yours, too?" Robin asked.

Henry pushed her away. "Jesus, Robin, I'm not the one who has something to hide."

"You sure? How are you going to explain that fat lip and beat-up hand?"

"Don't worry. I've got it covered."

"Then none of it ever happened and we're good to go?" Robin said.

"Maybe you are, if you're lucky," Henry said, "but I'm not done with it, and I doubt it's done with me."

TEN

By eight o'clock on Friday morning, the news that Peter Trout and three other rangers had located Jordan Groves spread through the hamlet like wildfire. It appeared that Groves had abandoned the Petty trail and panicked. Rather than retracing his tracks, he bushwhacked well over a quarter of a mile before falling to the bottom of a rock-studded ravine known as Adrian's Abyss. Ranger Trout said Grove's inexperience as a hiker was noteworthy. He wasn't carrying any water or a rain jacket, wore open-toed sandals, and not one but two killer-cotton items from Giorgio Armani: a pair of slim-fit trousers and a long-sleeve poplin shirt.

As soon as Julia heard the news, she rushed to her father's office and placed her hands on her knees to catch her breath. The Llewellins lifted their heads, thumped their tails once, and went back to sleep. "Guess what." She gasped. "They found the hiker."

Big Louis looked up from his *NY Times* and asked what in the Sam Hill she was talking about.

Julia drew a deep breath and gave her father a questioning look. "I'm talking about the hiker who went missing. Remember?"

"Of course. The one who went missing."

Julia straightened and flopped in the chair usually occupied by Owen. "Well, he's not missing anymore. They found him at the bottom of Adrian's Abyss."

"Lost or too steep for him to climb out?" Big Louis asked.

"Neither, actually. Too dead is more like it."

Big Louis didn't seem to register her comment and went back to reading.

Julia raised her voice. "Hello? Dad? It's your daughter, Julia, and I'm here to talk to you."

Her father spread the newspaper across his lap. "He's not the first victim of Adrian's Abyss. Owen says his great uncle bought the farm in the same spot back in the early twenties. He says they never really knew what happened, but lots of folks in the hamlet swore it had to be a murder."

"A good story, Dad, but one for another time." Julia paused for a moment. "Robin says she told you about our fence."

"She did, did she? And what, exactly, did she say she told me?"

Julia thought, *the well-rehearsed 'I'll pretend I remember and bait you into remembering for me' trick.* "She said she told you that we're planning on building a deer fence. But, knowing her, I'm guessing she didn't tell you that, thanks to global warming, there are lots of deer ticks in our area, and we're building the fence so our kids won't get Lyme disease."

Big Louis nodded and said he wouldn't want that for his little darlings.

Julia sighed a sigh of relief. "I knew you'd understand, Dad. You're such a good grandfather."

Big Louis smiled. "Those little darlings would have given your mother so much joy." He cleared his throat, flipped the page of his newspaper, and went back to reading.

"One other thing?" When her father looked up, Julia asked if Robin had told him about their easement or, rather, their lack of an easement.

"She mentioned something about it." Suddenly, Big Louis sat upright, closed his paper, and dropped it on the floor. "You don't have one. Right? And Owen says that wasn't what we agreed."

"Owen's right, but did Robin also tell you that she doesn't have one either?"

"Robin doesn't have one either? What the hell's gotten into all of you?" Big Louis bellowed. "Does that mean Eleanor doesn't have one?"

"You'll have to ask her," Julia said.

"Don't worry, I will, and I'm going to find a way to renege on our deal the way all of you have." He sat for a moment as though he was lost in thought, then got up and poured himself another coffee. "Now, if it's okay with you, I'd like some time to myself. To get things sorted out. My God, but the three of you certainly do complicate my life. At times it's like I don't even exist."

ELEVEN

Big Louis began what turned into a milestone session by asking Owen what was going on with his family, that Julia had told him that neither she nor Robin had eased their properties.

Knowing he was skating on thin ice, Owen hesitated and said Julia was right; only Eleanor had eased her property.

"Goddamn it, Owen, isn't that a breach of contract or something?"

"We've been through this before, Louis, a number of times. The problem is you never signed a formal agreement."

"So? Can I change my mind?"

Owen sighed. "Once again, Louis, I'm afraid not. They took title to their properties over three years ago."

"And I'm just finding out now?" Big Louis said. "Why didn't you tell me?"

"I did. I raised this issue with you before but didn't press it. I didn't think it was my place to get involved then, and I still don't."

"I don't know about you, Owen. I just don't know."

An uncomfortable silence followed. Finally, Big Louis said, "Those three are enough to drive a man to drink. Especially that Eleanor."

"Eleanor? I'd have guessed Robin or Julia way ahead of Eleanor. She's the only one to follow through on the easement deal."

"You taking Eleanor's side?" Big Louis asked.

Owen chuckled. "For Pete's sake, Louis, I don't even know what her side is."

"You sure?"

Owen said he was sure.

"So, Eleanor never talked to you about putting me in a home?"

"A home?"

"Yes, Owen, a home. The Cliffs."

"Not The Cliffs specifically, but she has shared her worries about someone your age living alone. And I think she's got a point; a place like The Cliffs is something you should consider; keep open as an option."

"So, you *are* on her side, and she does tell you everything!"

"Whoa, Louis. Hold up a minute—"

"No, you hold up a goddamned minute, Owen. I've let you in on every detail of my life, and now you're turning on me? What kind of friend are you?"

Owen told him that he was the best kind of friend: the kind that puts his friends' interests first.

"Well, no longer."

"What do you mean no longer?"

"I mean just that, no longer. I'm giving you your notice."

"Whoa!" Owen said. "You're firing me after twenty years over a simple misunderstanding? You can't be serious."

"I sure as hell am serious. Loyalty means everything to me, and you and Eleanor aren't watching my back. Now, do me a favor and get out of my sight."

Owen sat upright and turned his coffee cup in his hands. He tried to make what he was about to say sound like friendly advice. He thought this was just one of Big Louis' increasingly frequent outbursts, and he could talk him off the ledge. "Louis, I'm not talking behind your back. Never have; never will. You've been a great boss and a great friend, and all I've ever tried to do was what was best for you. That's the bottom line for me and Eleanor, too, so I'd think twice about this if I were you. Friends like me, especially ones with our long history and my loyalty and knowledge of your family's affairs, don't grow on trees."

"Is that a threat?"

Owen thought he'd give it one last try. "It is what it is, Louis. Certainly, not a threat. I'd like to think it's a piece of really good advice from someone who cares one hell of a lot about you and your family."

"Well, I'm not buying it," Big Louis said. "I'm done with you."

Owen stood and climbed over Sweetheart to leave. His hands were trembling as he set his cup next to the coffee maker. "Have it your way, but for starters, who are you going to get to replace me? Pickings in this neck of the woods are pretty slim, you know."

"Who knows," Big Louis said. "Maybe I'll do it all myself."

Owen shook his head and muttered, "Good God almighty."

As Owen left and closed the door behind him, Big Louis called after him: "I don't care what you or the girls think, I'm not over the hill, not ready for a home. Not by a goddamned long shot. I'll show you. I will. You can bet your sweet ass I will."

TWELVE

When darkness veiled the mountains and covered the valley floor, it seemed to take the edge off the recent events in the Honeywell household, and both Henry and Robin tried to hide their anxieties by keeping their discussions as neutral and good-humored as possible.

Henry set several armfuls of logs by the fireplace and called to Robin that the temperature was supposed to drop to near freezing before morning. As an afterthought, he added, "Oh, by the way, they found the missing hiker."

Robin called back from the kitchen, "Late, breaking news: supper will be ready by the time you've got the fire going."

"Great," Henry said and balled up pages from the *Lake Placid News* to set the fire. "Peter Trout thinks the poor bastard must have lost his way and stumbled into Adrian's Abyss. That's where the rangers found him, stone cold dead."

"What a horrible way to go," Robin said. "You can bet he was someone who wasn't familiar with the mountains."

Henry spread some fatwood on the crumpled newspaper and set a few logs in place. "Go to the head of the class. He was from Greenwich, of all places."

Robin emerged from the kitchen, drying her hands with a dishtowel. "Greenwich? Are you sure?"

"Positive. They found his car and his license."

Robin grabbed the back of the sofa with both hands. "Did Peter tell you his name?"

"Yeah. Something or other Groves."

The color drained from Robin's face. "Jordan Groves?" Before Henry could ask how she knew the guy's name Robin fainted dead away, pulling a lamp made from a carving of a loon to the floor with her.

Henry rushed to her and asked if she was okay. Robin's eyes fluttered, but she didn't respond. He grabbed the dish towel she was clutching, ran to the kitchen, and soaked it in cold water. When he returned, Robin was still lying on the floor, mumbling, "What about my forty-five grand? What about my forty-five grand?"

Henry knelt beside her, lifted her head, pressed the cold dish towel to her forehead, and told her to stay put and relax. As the color returned to her face, Henry helped her to the couch and sat beside her. "Better?"

"Getting there."

"You feel well enough to talk?"

Robin lay back and stretched her legs across his lap. "If we must."

He asked how she recognized the hiker's name and why it upset her, and what was with the forty grand?

"Forty-five," Robin said. "Jordan Groves is the guy who I did that mega-deal with in Upper St. Regis. You know, the guy who was . . . was . . . visiting when you came home."

Henry lifted her legs from across his lap and stood. "Jesus, Robin, you may call that the ultimate in customer satisfaction, but I've got other names for it, like breaking the heart of someone who loves you very much."

Robin began to sob. "How many times and how many ways can I say I'm sorry?" She paused and reached for his hand. The color had left her face again, and she said she felt a little nauseous. After a moment, she said, "No matter how hard I try, I can't undo it, Honeybunch. What's done is done. What's more, just before you interrupted us, I panicked, knowing that I'd made a huge mistake and was beginning to chicken out. Like I said, nothing really happened. One thing's for sure; I'll never do that again."

"You promise there haven't been others?" Henry said.

"I swear to God, on a stack of bibles," Robin said.

"Okay," Henry said and sat back down. "I'll have to live with that, I guess."

"My turn?" Robin asked.

Henry nodded.

"What happened between you and Jordan after you chased him from the house?"

Henry began to answer when the kitchen alarm started screeching and dark smoke wafted into the living room.

"Oh, shit, the burgers," Robin said. "The fucking hamburgers." As she struggled to get up and staggered to the kitchen, she screamed, "Jesus, Henry, bring the fire extinguisher! On the double."

Once Henry had extinguished the flames engulfing the hamburgers, he opened the kitchen windows to clear the smoke while Robin scraped the charred burgers from the frying pan onto a plate. She said she'd seen worse but couldn't remember when or where. She took a deep breath to regain her composure and was about to ask again what had happened between Jordan and him when she was interrupted by someone at the kitchen door. "Jesus, Honeybunch, it's a cop. And a black one at that. He's not looking for you, is he?"

Henry shrugged. "Let me handle it."

The state trooper introduced himself as Sgt. Oswald and asked if he was speaking with Mr. Honeywell. "The one and only," Henry said and laughed. "Come on in, Sarge. We were just burning the house down."

Once inside, the trooper took off his flat-brimmed Stetson, nodded at Robin, and said that he had some questions for the two of them about a man named Jordan Groves.

"Who?" Henry asked.

"The hiker the rangers found at the bottom of Adrian's Abyss," Sgt. Oswald said.

Henry nodded. "And his name was Jordan Groves?"

"Yes, sir. And, Mrs. Honeywell, I understand you knew him."

Robin flushed. "I can't believe it. We'd just closed on the purchase of a property in Upper St. Regis last week. And . . ." She paused.

"And what, ma'am?" the trooper asked.

"Well, to be perfectly honest with you, I'm wondering if I'm going to be paid my commission. It's my biggest deal ever."

"And when did you last see Mr. Groves?"

"Monday. At the closing in Saranac Lake."

"Not since?"

"Not since. A deal's a deal, and then I move on. All I care about now is my forty-five—"

"I understand," Sgt. Oswald interrupted. "But, just a couple of more questions, ma'am. Do you have any idea what he was doing on the Petty trail?"

"Hiking, I would guess. He talked a lot about how much he loved our mountains and how much he'd love to become part of them."

"Well, in a way, he got his wish," Henry said, then hurriedly added, "I mean, not the way he wanted it, of course."

"That's for sure," Sgt. Oswald said. He directed his next question to Henry, pointing to his swollen lip. "What happened there?"

"Caught my wading shoe on a root and took a header over on the west branch." Henry held up his injured hand. "Broke my fall with this and my mouth."

"When did that happen?" the trooper asked.

"Last Wednesday, on Robin's—on my wife's—birthday."

"The day Mr. Groves went missing," the trooper said.

"If you say so," Henry said.

"You were in Levi Lamb that day?"

"For sure. I was here to celebrate Robin's big four-oh."

"Jesus, Henry, you could have spared that detail," Robin said.

"And you celebrated your wife's birthday by going fishing?" the sergeant asked.

"That a crime? She was showing a new listing up on Rocky Peak Lane, so I took a few hours to wet a line."

The trooper smiled for the first time since he'd arrived. "Not a crime in my books." He looked at Robin. "Were you showing the property on Rocky Peak to a Mrs. Forsythe?"

"Yes, but how did . . ." Robin hesitated.

Sgt. Oswald said it was all part of putting the pieces together for the Groves investigation.

"Investigation?" Henry asked.

"Yes, sir. We're trying to determine if there was any foul play." The trooper paused for a second as though he was ordering his thoughts and then asked Henry if anyone was with him.

"Was anyone with me when?" Henry asked.

"The afternoon you hurt your lip."

"No," Henry said. "I like to fish by myself. You know, the solitude of the great outdoors and all that good stuff."

"No one saw you fall? Another fisherman, perhaps?"

"I don't think so," Henry said, "but then again, I wasn't there for very long."

"Got it," Sgt. Oswald said. He handed his card to Henry and asked him to call if he or Mrs. Honeywell happened to think of anything else that he should know about Mr. Groves. He turned to leave, nodded goodbye to Robin, but stopped short of the door. "Mrs. Honeywell, I don't think I'd eat those burgers if I were you. Not a police order but a friendly suggestion."

After Sgt. Oswald left, Robin gave Henry a troubled look. "Foul play? You don't think he suspects that you had something to do with Jordan's death? That you may have—" Her eyes widened. "Oh, Jesus, Henry, you don't think the police know about Jordan and me, and that's why they're so interested in you?"

"How in the world could they? No one knows about you and Jordan except the two of us."

"Right . . . Well, no . . . I mean . . . I mean, there may be someone else," Robin said.

Henry picked up a fork and sampled one of the hamburgers. "Someone else?"

"Frisky Forsythe was on the phone when Jordan showed up. I was so surprised by his presence I may have called him by name."

Henry choked on a charred bite of hamburger. "Think, Robin. Think, Goddamnit, think. Did you, or didn't you?"

Robin looked away. After a moment, almost in a whisper, she said, "I can't say for sure, but I'm afraid I did."

"Of course, you did. That's why Sgt. Oswald was here. There's no two ways about it." Henry sat on a stool by the kitchen island and rested his head in his hands. "How else would he know that you were showing Frisky a property if she hadn't heard Jordan's name and called the police?"

Robin began to cry. "Oh, Jesus, Honeybunch."

"And Frisky Forsythe of all people," Henry said. "If she told the police, by now she's told half the town. Can you see what you've done?"

"Of course," Robin said. "Of course, I can. I'm not that stupid. And along with it, now I'm the town whore. So, what more do you want? You and the townies to burn me at the stake?"

"For God's sake, Robin, get a grip. I'm the one being questioned about that bastard's death, not you."

"Well, if you hadn't fought with him and chased him, maybe none of this would have happened."

"Wrong. Dead wrong. You're the villain here, clear and simple. So, don't try to pass the buck to me."

"Well, how do you explain Jordan's death if I'm the only villain?" Robin asked. "I mean, really, Henry, what did happen?"

"Your guess is as good as mine. He must have stumbled into Adrian's Abyss."

"Stumbled or was pushed?"

Henry stood, grabbed his car keys, and started toward the kitchen door.

"Are you walking out to avoid telling me the truth?" Robin asked.

Henry reached for the door handle, then stopped. "You want the truth? Well, here's the truth. You put me in one hell of a spot, and I reacted the way any normal husband would. And the hardest part of all is that I don't think I can live with you after what you've done to me. That's the truth, the bigger truth. Simple as that. And now I'm going somewhere to eat something that doesn't remind me of what a home-wrecker you are."

THIRTEEN

In most ways, Julia was as different from her father as night is from day. With Julia, her loving, soft side was on display 24/7 while Big Louis worked hard to keep his feelings under wraps for fear of looking weak. For him, appearances were all that mattered.

But, in other ways, the apple hadn't fallen far from the tree. A case in point: in the same manner that her father used to say goodnight to Julia and her sisters when they were youngsters, Julia followed a similar routine every night as she put her kids to bed, although she preferred to call it a *ritual*, not a *routine*. To her, a "routine" sounded too impersonal, while a ritual sounded more like something that connected the kids to the sacred, whatever or whoever that might be. She wanted them to believe in something unimaginable, something filled with goodness and love, something that encouraged them to be kind to others and themselves.

The ritual started with her children giving a goodnight hug and kiss to Ravi and Jeter, with "love yous" all around. Next, her daughters moved a menagerie of stuffed bears, rabbits, and monkeys out of their way and got into their shiny cedar log bunk bed. Hansi, nine, climbed the ladder to the top bunk where she thought she could see the whole universe from her window. Sara, seven, chose the bottom bunk just in case she wanted to crawl into bed with Julia and Ravi in the middle of the night.

Kasun, twelve, retired to his man cave with its aspen mission bed that looked like beavers had assembled it from the way the logs were whittled down at their ends. A Yankees flag that listed the 27 years they'd won the World Series hung above Kasun's bureau, to which his grandfather often asked, "Do we really need to be reminded of that?" Jeter's camouflaged bed was nestled in a corner of Kasun's thickly carpeted room and personalized with a bold #2 to honor the Yankees' legendary shortstop. It was only for show because Jeter slept on Kasun's bed every night, and no one in the family wanted to end what Kasun called "the Jeter streak."

This night, Julia called from the hall, "All nestled down and ready for some sweet dreams?" She waited for a second, then said: "Everybody, take a deep breath." Another pause, then: "Hansi, a loving-kindness prayer?"

"May I treat others the way I want to be treated."

"Kasun?"

"May I be strong but not be a bully."

"Sara?"

"May I be safe and happy."

Hansi said, "That doesn't count. You can't pray for two things."

"Why not if it's what I want?" Sara asked.

"I think when you need to double down, you can," Julia said. "I may do that tonight." When the issue seemed to have been resolved, Julia said, "May I be healthy and unafraid," and asked if anyone needed to pray for help, or give thanks, or had a "wow!";

the three essential prayers of Anne Lamott, her favorite writer and "way-shower."

The girls didn't offer anything, but Kasun said, "I have a 'wow!' for Aunt Robin. She saw a Bicknell's thrush in her garden, and Mr. Gill told our class that that's a huge deal because there aren't many of them left in the Adirondacks. So that's my 'wow!'"

"That's a 'wow!' for sure," Julia said. "A 'wow' for Aunt Robin and a 'wow!' for you for thinking so lovingly of her." She watched as the lights in the bedrooms clicked off. "Tonight, I need help. Help to be strong with a problem that I can't solve by myself."

The kids didn't respond, and she went to all three and kissed them goodnight and told them how much she loved them.

Ravi was stationed in front of the TV, watching the Yankees thrash the Orioles when Julia joined him. He patted his thighs, inviting her to sit in his lap. "You okay?" he asked. "You seem somewhere else tonight."

Julia sat and held him by his shoulders, then bit her lower lip and began to sob.

"Whoa," Ravi said. "What's going on?"

"All that stuff with the specialist in Burlington? Well, it isn't bleeding from hemorrhoids. Dr. Ritter says that I'm a very healthy woman with a very big problem." She paused and wiped at her tears. "Oh my God, Ravi, I don't know if I can even say it."

Ravi punched off the TV. "Say it. I'm right here."

Julia sighed. "I've got rectal cancer, and it's pretty far along."

"Why didn't you—"

"I didn't want to worry you until I'd seen the oncologist. Even now, I can't believe it."

Ravi pulled her to him as she heaved with tears, releasing all her self-control, disbelief, fears, and anger. "It's like it's happening to someone else. I'm so scared that I can't think of anything else."

"You'll whip it. I know you will." Ravi held her tighter. "We'll whip it. Together. No matter what it takes. What's the prognosis? I mean—"

"No numbers, Ravi. Please, don't ask for percentages. I've researched it on the internet but was afraid to ask Dr. Ritter about my chances. All I know is that it can kill me, and all she talked about was how she planned to treat me and make me well again. It all sounds so horrible, and there's no guarantee."

"What would your way-shower say?" Ravi asked. "Bird by bird? Well, we'll take it bird by bird, Julia. Together. You and me. As a team. I promise. Nothing will get in our way."

Julia and Ravi agreed that Ravi should tell their kids about her cancer because Julia knew she'd fall apart in front of them if she tried, just adding to their worries. And Ravi volunteered to spare her from telling her father because neither of them knew quite how he would react.

Ravi chose to tell Big Louis first, kind of a mixture of sending a pig through a minefield to see if it became instant pork chops and a dress rehearsal for his talk with his kids. He knocked lightly on the door to his father-in-law's office and waited for him to look up from his morning paper. When he realized that the old man had dozed off, Ravi cleared his throat and said, "Mr. McCutchen?"

Big Louis woke with a start and stared blankly at him. When he registered who it was, he asked, "To what do I owe this honor?"

"Sorry to bother you, sir," Ravi said, "but I'd like a word with you if I could."

"Of course. Of course. Come on in. Just catching up on the Sox."

Ravi slowly shut the door behind him. The Llewellins raised their heads, thumped their tails a few times, and lay back on their beds as Ravi reached to shake Big Louis' hand. "It's nice to see you, sir."

"You, too." Big Louis pointed to the chair that for so many years had been occupied primarily by Owen. "Make yourself at home."

As Ravi sat, Big Louis asked if he followed the Red Sox.

Ravi forced a smile. "I know you're kidding, Mr. McCutchen. Nothing's changed on that score. Kasun and I are still dyed-in-the-wool Yankees fans."

His father-in-law reacted as though it was news to him. "You, I can understand, not being from here and all of that. But Kasun? I thought that little ankle-biter was perfect. Oh, well, live and learn. And how are the girls?"

"They're fine, really great, and thanks for asking. It's Julia I'd like to talk to you about."

Big Louis folded his newspaper and dropped it on the floor. "Don't tell me you're getting a divorce. You know we've never had a divorce in the McCutchen family."

"Not to worry, Mr. McCutchen. That's not the issue," Ravi said. "Far from it. We've never been happier, but we've just received some very bad news about Julia's health. She wanted to tell you herself but didn't think she had the strength and asked me to talk with you instead." He hesitated for a moment. "Julia has colorectal cancer, an extremely troublesome kind of cancer."

Big Louis shrugged. "What cancer isn't troublesome?"

Ravi agreed that all cancers were troublesome, but some were more difficult to treat than others.

Big Louis raised his bushy white eyebrows. "Well, at least it's treatable. The doctors in Boston said that there was nothing they could do to save Katherine."

"I understand, sir. That must have been a very, very sad time for you and your family."

"How could you understand?" Big Louis asked. "You never even met Katherine."

"No, sir, but the love you and Julia and her sisters have for her is still all around us."

Big Louis didn't respond and picked his newspaper from the floor. "Have you talked with Sandy Janeway about this? Maybe he knows what to do."

"We've consulted with Dr. Janeway every step of the way. He's been a great help."

"So, Sandy's in charge?"

Ravi wanted to tell his father-in-law that he didn't seem to understand that Julia's cancer was a life-or-death proposition that demanded a team of sophisticated specialists in a hospital setting but thought better of it. "Dr. Janeway's opened a lot of doors and put us in touch with a number of specialists."

"It was the so-called specialists who couldn't help Katherine, so be careful."

"I understand, sir, and we're being as careful as we can. We've chosen the University of Vermont Cancer Center so Julia can be close to the kids. And she likes the oncologist who's been treating her, even though she told Julia that she was going to throw the kitchen sink at her to cure her, meaning that the treatment is going to be long and painful."

Ravi waited for Big Louis to say something, but he simply stared at the floor. Finally, Ravi asked when he would pay Julia a call.

"A call?" Big Louis said. "Of course, a call. It seems like all I do these days is fight uphill battles with my daughters, but tell her I'll be in touch soon."

Ravi stared at a copy of *Barron's* without absorbing a word he was reading while he waited for his two older kids to finish their homework. When he thought the time had come, his heart began to race. Over the years, he'd made countless presentations to captains of industry and demanding financial analysts from Wall Street to The City in London, but thought what he was about to do was the most stressful and by far the most important talk he'd ever given. He raised a shaking hand, put two fingers in his mouth, and whistled. "Team meeting. Everybody on deck and on the double."

The girls curled in his lap the way their mother always did while Kasun sat on the ottoman between his feet and Jeter turned in circles before lying close to his human pack. Ravi massaged Sara's neck, reached for Hansi's hand, and silently prayed for strength. Tears built behind his eyes when Hansi asked, "Where's Mommy?"

Ravi told her that their mommy was finishing up in the kitchen, that she'd be with them in a minute.

And then, he began.

"Everybody feeling strong?"

The kids seemed confused because that was their mother's type of question, not their father's. They looked at one another and nodded.

"Everybody filled with love?"

All nodded again.

"Good, good, and good," Ravi said and drew a deep breath. "So, here's the deal: Mommy is sick and must go to the hospital to get well." He paused, waiting for a question, but the kids just sat straighter and again looked at one another, perhaps for understanding, definitely for strength. "Mommy has cancer, and it will take her a long time to get better."

"Is Mommy going to die?" Sara asked.

"Sara," Kasun said, "don't be a brat."

"No, no. It's alright, Sara, and it's okay, Kasun. All questions are okay. That's the first thing everybody wants to know when they hear that someone has cancer. It's such a scary word. But, no, Mommy's not going to die. She's young and strong and loves us and loves life. She's going to need our help for a long, long time, but she's going to beat her cancer and live."

"Promise?" Hansi said.

Ravi said that it was going to be a struggle, but she'd be okay.

"Promise, Daddy? Promise?" Hansi asked again.

Ravi hesitated.

"This sucks," Kasun said. "He won't promise because he can't."

Ravi leaned forward and pulled all three close to him. He could feel their sobs and fought not to join them. "At the start, when people are very sick, no one can promise anything. That's one of the hard parts about this. But the odds are in Mommy's favor, and we'll do everything we can to make her well."

"And you'll stay in our house with us?" Sara asked.

"Of course," Ravi said. "And much of the time, Mommy will be here too, so you can help her get well. So, for now, we love and pray and hope and talk whenever we're scared. Whenever we need to."

The children didn't ask any more questions; they just tightened their circle, getting as close as possible to one another and their father.

FOURTEEN

Big Louis was kneeling on the floor, brushing the Llewellins, when Eleanor peered into his office. "Dad, you got a minute?"

"I guess," Big Louis said and slowly worked his way to his feet. "Unless it's more nonsense about your easements or locking me up in some goddamned home. I've had enough of all of that."

Eleanor shut the door and reached for her father's hands. "Well then, how about a kiss to start the day off right?" She pecked him on the cheek and turned him toward his favorite chair. "Coffee?"

"Cream, but no sugar."

Eleanor smiled. She had made coffee for her father too many times to count since her mother's death, and each and every time he told her he took his coffee with cream but no sugar.

Once he was seated, Eleanor handed him his cup and sat in the chair opposite him.

Big Louis sipped his coffee, then asked, "To what do I owe this honor?"

"I've got some stuff that I'd like to talk with you about that I hope will clear the air."

"Clear the air? Now, what are you talking about? You not having a boyfriend?"

Eleanor ignored his comment, but the way her father said "Now what are you talking about," prepared her for what was sure to come. She leaned toward him. "Let's start with Julia's fence and the easements on our properties."

"No." Big Louis waved his hands. "No, no, no. There's nothing more to talk about. I gave the three of you those parcels with the understanding that you'd conserve them, and every damn one of you has gone back on your word."

"Wrong, Dad, and that's one of the reasons why I wanted to talk with you. Robin hasn't eased her property because she thinks it will reduce its value, and she's convinced Julia and Ravi not to ease theirs either. That's their issue, not mine, so pay attention here: I eased my property as soon as I took title, just the way I said I would. Just the way you wanted me to."

Her father asked if Owen knew that.

"Of course, Owen knows it," Eleanor said. "And he says he's discussed it with you a number of times."

Big Louis shook his head. "He never told me. I should have fired him long ago."

"That's another thing I wanted to talk about. After all these years, why in the world did you fire him? Owen, of all people. He's your best—"

"Because you and he talked about me behind my back, and . . . and he sided with you about putting me in a home."

"Dad, please, we only discussed what we thought would be best for you. You know, like people who care about you? Who love you?"

"That's a bunch of baloney. You and he wanted to get me off your hands, and you know it. So, I fired the son of a bitch, and if I could, I'd fire you, too. I should have quit with two kids."

Her father had never attacked her personally before, and Eleanor didn't know what to say. Finally, she said, "You don't mean that, and you know it." She waited for his reply, but Big Louis simply stared at her. "Or do you?"

"You're damn right, I mean it." He struggled to get up and took a step toward Eleanor, pointing a finger at her. "I've always demanded loyalty from the people who work for me and from my family, and you and Owen have let me down when I needed you the most."

"Dad, relax. Please. We're all here for you. Owen and I, and Julia and Robin, too. We'll do anything for you. All we want is for you to be happy. Safe and happy."

"On your terms, not mine," Big Louis said. "Well, to hell with you and your other agenda items, this meeting's over."

Eleanor stood. Tears filled her eyes as she opened the door. "I think I know what you're going through, Dad, and think it must be tough as hell. Growing old has to be difficult to accept, especially for a man like you who expects so much of himself. If there's ever any way I can help, just let me know. I love you, and, no matter what you say or do, that will never change."

Big Louis slammed the door behind his once-favorite daughter and looked down at the Llewellins. *How in hell would she know what I'm going through? She and her sisters have no idea what it's like being in a broken-down old body like mine. Balance shot to hell. Have to fight to get out of a chair and can barely read my handwriting. Not even strong enough to open the cellophane in the Wheaties box, for God's sake. No, they've got no idea what's in store for them. No goddamn idea at all.*

He moved to the window that looked out at the slides on Dix Mountain. Storm clouds were building in the distance, and the maples were beginning to change color. He placed his once powerful hands, now liver-spotted with crooked fingers and swollen knuckles, on either side of the window frame and pressed his forehead against the cool glass. *My daughters, the queens of easy street. Think they know everything and think I don't know what's happening, that all of this will go away if I move into that goddamned prison. Well, to hell with them. All three of them. I do know what's happening. I'm caught between bases, between the man I used to be and a pathetic old man who's lost everything. Lost the only woman I ever loved. And all respect. All stature. I haven't got a friend in the world except for three bird dogs. Well, I'm not ready to quit, no matter what they think.*

He turned and slowly lowered himself to his knees and then to all fours. The Llewellins stood and, wagging their tails, nuzzled their master's neck and licked the tears from his cheeks.

"It's all right, dogs," Big Louis said. "It has to be. There's only one other way out, and I'm not there yet."

FIFTEEN

Sandy Janeway studied the Llewellins, reciting their names in soothing tones to entertain himself while he waited for Big Louis to look up from the newspaper. Finally, he said, "It's too bad we can't raise our kids to behave as well as your dogs."

Big Louis laughed from behind the newspaper. "Maybe everyone should use shock collars."

The doctor smiled but said that this was no time for jokes, that he needed to talk to Big Louis about a couple of family issues.

"Got it," Big Louis said, "but first, let me ask you a question: you a baseball fan?"

"Yes, Louis, but —"

"Good, because I don't understand the way things are reported anymore. Do we have a chance of making the playoffs, or don't we?"

Sandy drew a deep breath; the last thing he wanted to do was talk baseball. "If by 'we' you mean the Red Sox, they don't have a snowball's prayer in hell."

"How can you be so goddamned sure? You sound like a Yankees fan."

"Because, when you're in the cellar, fifteen games out of first with only seven games left, there's no way you're going to make the playoffs."

"Well, I'll be damned," Big Louis said. "Doesn't seem like we ever get to the World Series anymore."

Sandy reminded him that the Sox had won the Series in 2013, just two years ago. When Big Louis didn't respond and his vacant stare indicated that he'd lost the thread of the conversation, the doctor said, "Okay? Down to family business?"

Big Louis shrugged.

"I'd like to bring you up to date on Julia's situation," Sandy said.

"If it's about her Goddamned fence, no dice."

"Good God no, Louis, it's not about her fence. It's a medical report, and a bit of a caution."

Big Louis signaled impatiently for the doctor to deliver his message.

"The good news is that her radiation went very well. With that behind her, in a couple of weeks she'll be operated on and then begin her chemotherapy." He paused. "You with me so far?"

Big Louis nodded. "Of course."

"Good, because here's the part that I want you to concentrate on. The chemo regimen will be one infusion every two weeks for close to six months, and its side effects can become a living hell."

"That bad?"

"Worse than you can imagine."

Big Louis ran his hand across his cheeks and his chin and nodded.

"So here's the bottom line, Louis: so far, so good. But please, please give Julia all the love and support you can. She's going to need it. And so are Ravi and the kids." He reached a hand toward Big Louis and gently gripped his forearm. "Now, for the hard part."

"More about Julia?"

"Nope, it's about Robin. Man to man. Between old friends. Okay?"

"More about that goddamned fence?" Big Louis asked.

"No, Louis. This is kind of like a doctor with his patient."

"Not The Cliffs again."

Sandy shook his head. "I'm not sure I should be telling you this, but rumor has it that Henry caught Robin having sex with a customer. Frisky Forsythe's spread it all over town, and I thought you should be aware."

"My Robin?"

"Yes, your Robin."

"You sure?"

"I'm pretty damn sure. The police are looking into it right now."

Big Louis pulled his arm from Sandy's grasp. "Since when has it been a crime to have sex with a customer?"

"It wasn't just any customer. It was the hiker Peter Trout found at the bottom of Adrian's Abyss."

"And what's he got to say about it?"

"Who? Peter Trout?" Sandy asked.

"No, the hiker. The customer."

"He's not talking—"

"I'll bet he isn't," Big Louis interrupted. "Typical of a goddamned liar."

"Maybe," Sandy said. "But in this case, he's not talking because he can't. He was dead when the rangers found him. Remember?"

Big Louis looked surprised. "Some guy died in Adrian's Abyss?"

"Yes. Some guy died in Adrian's Abyss."

"Why are you telling me this?"

"Now, I'm not really sure," Sandy said and stood to leave. "I just wanted you to know that there's an ugly rumor going around town about one of your daughters, and I didn't want you to be caught off guard."

"About Robin?"

"Yes, Louis, about your Robin."

"I don't put much stock in rumors, but I'll ask her about it."

"I wouldn't if I were you. Let her work through it on her own." Sandy gave his old friend a salute. "And, if it's okay with you, I'll check in again in a couple of days to see how you're doing."

SIXTEEN

Henry was crouching in front of the Hodgepodge's cereal section, restocking and rearranging the Wheaties and the Cheerios, when he felt a gentle tap on his shoulder. Without looking up, he said, "How can I help you?"

A familiar voice, but one that Henry couldn't place, answered, "I need a minute of your time, Mr. Honeywell. If you would, sir."

Henry turned to face a pair of highly polished black oxford shoes beneath sharply pressed gray trousers accented with a black stripe. Still crouched, he reached up to shake Sgt. Oswald's hand. "Welcome to the Hodgepodge, Sarge. Can I help you find something?"

The trooper asked if there was a place where they could talk. Privately.

Henry stood and slipped his work apron over his head. "It's a beautiful fall day. How about a little walk?"

Sgt. Oswald shook his head. "Not private enough. Isn't there someplace here? In the store?"

Henry laughingly suggested the cold room.

Sgt. Oswald surprised him by saying that sounded perfect.

"Perfect?" Henry said. "We're talking cold, like thirty-four degrees, Sarge."

The trooper smiled. "Okay by me, if it's okay by you. Besides, this won't take but a minute."

Once inside the well-lighted refrigerated room, Henry began to explain: "This is where we keep our dairy products, vegetables, and meats. I've developed an efficient First In, First Out—"

Sgt. Oswald interrupted him. "If you would, sir, save that for another time. I'd like to ask you a few more questions about the day Mr. Groves was reported missing."

"Sorry, Sarge, but I'm afraid I've told you all I know."

"Maybe, maybe not. Think about it real hard, Mr. Honeywell. Are you sure no one saw you fall on the river bank the day in question?"

"Yes, officer, I'm sure. There was no one else fishing." Henry paused. "As I've told you, I wasn't there for very long, only long enough to do my clumsy face plant."

"Roger that," Sgt. Oswald said. "I'm a golfer, so let me ask you kind of an ignorant question about fishing: do you cast right- or left-handed?"

"Cast right, reel left. I learned that from—"

"And, what hand do you carry your rod in?"

Henry moved his hands from side to side. "Aren't you cold? You've got goosebumps on your forearms."

"I'm fine, thanks, Mr. Honeywell. Just answer the question, please."

"Usually, my right," Henry said.

"So, you banged up your right hand pretty badly when you fell but didn't break your rod? Don't you find that a little odd?"

"Lucky maybe, but not odd. I tried to break my fall with my hand."

"Even though you had your rod in it?"

"A reflex action, Sarge. As I'm sure you understand, I didn't have much time to think about what I was doing."

Sgt. Oswald said, "Got it," and drew a small notebook from his shirt pocket and wrote something in it.

"I'm not sure why you're asking me all these questions; what you're trying to get at," Henry said.

"Someone in the hamlet is claiming that you and Mr. Groves may have had a run-in on the day in question."

"Who's spreading that nonsense?"

Sgt. Oswald ignored Henry's question and told him that he was trying to determine if foul play was involved in the case.

"What makes you think there's foul play involved just because. . . ."

"Because what, sir?"

"That guy Groves fell into Adrian's Abyss? He's not the first person to end up at the bottom of that ravine."

"I understand, Mr. Honeywell, but we're following all leads to make sure we've investigated every angle."

"Every angle? For God's sake, Sarge, I've told you exactly what happened. What more can I do?"

"Well, there is one more thing," the trooper said. "I'd like to collect a sample of your DNA."

"You've got to be kidding."

Sgt. Oswald said the time for kidding had long passed.

Henry asked what would happen if he refused.

The sergeant said he had a court order for him to comply.

"And just where would I comply?" Henry asked.

"The kit's in my cruiser," Sgt. Oswald said. "It only takes a minute. A couple of cheek swabs, drop the tube in the evidence bag, and we're done."

Henry shrugged. "Why the hell not? Besides, I'm freezing my ass off."

SEVENTEEN

Robin woke early, intent upon bringing Henry back into the fold the best way she knew how. She slipped off her nightgown and rolled over to mount him, only to find that Henry's side of the bed was empty. She called for him to come back to bed, that she had a special treat for him, but he didn't answer. She called again. "Honeybunch, come and get it."

Still no answer.

She hurried to the kitchen, excited by the way the cool morning air caressed her naked body. She was sure that Henry would be there as he was every morning, feeding Goldilocks and enjoying his first cup of coffee, but there wasn't a sign of him or their retriever. She sensed that something wasn't quite right, and an uneasy feeling of emptiness came over her. She crossed her arms across her breasts to cover herself as if someone might be watching her when she was brought up short by an envelope on the kitchen table with *Gone Fishing* written on it in large red letters. She tore the envelope open and unfolded the single piece of paper inside it. The note read:

Robin -

By the time you read this, I will be out of your life FOREVER, so don't bother to try to find me because you won't be able to. I guess I loved you too much and won't ever be able to get over how much you've hurt and disappointed me. And the inevitable publicity of your affair will be devastating and embarrassing for us both, certainly more than I can endure. Please explain to Louis and Hobey what happened, so they'll understand why I've left, and tell them how much I love them and that I'll be in touch when the time is right. Give your father my regards and thank him for all he's done for me. And give my love to Eleanor, and especially Julia, and tell her that I wish her the very best with her surgery and her treatment and that she'll be in my prayers.

I hope you find what you're looking for in life.

HCH Jr.

P.S. Goldi is with me.

"What the fuck?" Robin screamed. "He can't be serious. After nineteen years he up and leaves me? And takes my darling Goldilocks in the bargain?" She dropped the note on the table and stared through the kitchen window at the yellow, red, and orange leaves that were beginning to cover the lawn. *Change everywhere, and now this. It's going to be one long, lonely fucking winter.*

She walked to her office to see if Henry had left a message on her answering machine. *No dice.* She sat in her desk chair and swiveled it back and forth. *He's doing this to punish me. To expose me. To take the spotlight off him, off of his problem. And what does he mean I won't be able to find him? Where could he possibly go? Well, if I can't find him, the police surely will.*

With jumbled thoughts running through her mind, Robin dressed and raced to the Hodgepodge, wondering, *What the hell do I tell Dad? And poor, sick Julia? And reliable Eleanor? And sweet Little Louis and Hobey?*

The door to Big Louis' office was open when Robin arrived. Still in a state of confusion, all she could think about was how her father would react to her news. *Head on*, she thought. *That's what he'd tell me. Take it head-on. That's the McCutchen way.* She began talking before crossing the threshold, but the office was empty. As she turned to leave, she collided with her father, who enfolded her in a bear hug. "Oh, thank God you're here," she said.

Big Louis held her for a moment and asked his well-rehearsed question, "To what do I owe this honor?"

Caught off guard by the torrent of tears that followed, at first, Robin didn't answer. Once she had her sobbing under control, she said it wasn't an honor and collapsed into what used to be Owen's chair. "Quite the opposite of an honor, actually, Dad. More like a dishonor."

Big Louis closed the door, leaned against it, and crossed his arms across his chest. "Something wrong?"

Robin ran her hands through her curls and looked up at him. "You'd better believe there's something wrong. Very, very wrong. Has Henry been in today?"

Big Louis said that he hadn't seen him, that he most probably was fishing.

"You can say that again."

Big Louis lowered himself into his chair. "Okay. What's bothering you?"

Robin wiped at her cheeks. "Dad, please don't be angry with me, okay?"

Her father shrugged. "It depends."

And it all poured out.

"Well, I've made a horrible, horrible mistake. Henry was away fishing on my birthday, and I guess I was hurt and not feeling loved. Maybe I was trying to get back at him for not paying enough attention to me. Maybe I was worried that I was getting old, that I'd lost my sex appeal. I don't know, but I was . . . was . . . physically intimate with some guy when Henry came home to surprise me. Nothing really happened between the guy and me, and it was the only time I've even come close to doing something like that, but Henry can't, or won't, forgive me, and he's left me."

"So, it's true," Big Louis said.

"What's true?"

"The rumor."

Robin panicked. "There's a rumor going around about me? Who told you? Is Henry involved?"

Big Louis struggled to get up from his chair and poured himself a cup of coffee. "It's okay. It's only a rumor."

"Only a rumor! Jesus, Dad, only a rumor? *Please* try to remember. You must. What are people saying?"

"Just like what you told me. Isn't that enough?"

"Is a guy named Jordan Groves involved? Maybe even the police?"

Big Louis said he didn't think so. He sat, slipped his glasses in his shirt pocket, and looked over his coffee cup at Robin. "So the little half-pint left you. You know we've never had a divorce in the McCutchen family."

Robin straightened in her chair and tried to compose herself but couldn't. "I give up. Fucking give up, Dad. The little half-pint, as you call him, is as big a man as you are. He isn't perfect, but he's the only man I've ever loved, and he's been a loyal husband and a great father to our boys. A divorce is the least of my problems. Or Henry's. Or, in a way, yours and the rest of our family. The real issues are my reputation, my shame, my sense of guilt, and how my sons will deal with this." She stood and leaned forward to kiss her father goodbye on the forehead but stopped. "I'm sorry, Dad, but if you don't understand that, you don't understand a thing I'm talking about. What's more, you'd better start listening to what Julia, Eleanor, and I are trying to tell you because, among other things, we're trying to save you from yourself."

Within the hour, Robin met with her sisters at her house, *her fucking empty nest*. She adopted her chairperson's persona and told them what she'd told their father and reported on his reaction.

Julia, who would be undergoing surgery in less than a week, was distracted by her medical problems but worked hard to stay involved in the conversation. Mostly, though, she held her big sister's hand and cried, praying that it all would work out.

Eleanor predicted that Henry would come to his senses and, maybe with a good therapist, he'd forgive Robin and move on if for no other reason than for their sons.

Robin surprised her sisters when she said, "But, that's far from the whole story."

Eleanor and Julia looked at one another and then back at Robin and asked what she meant by that.

"Here's what I think pushed Henry over the edge, made him run away," Robin said. "It's not to say what I did wasn't wrong or that I don't understand why it hurt him so, but there's more to it than just the sex, which, mind you, never really happened. When Henry surprised us, Jordan punched him and ran out of the house. I tried to stop Henry, but he caught Jordan on the driveway and hit him a couple of times and then chased him toward the Petty trail."

"You're not blaming Henry for being angry, are you?" Eleanor asked.

"I'm not blaming him for anything, Babycakes. I know I was in the wrong. But, in a heartbeat, a New York State Trooper came sniffing around, asking Henry and me a lot of questions about Jordan Groves, saying that he was trying to determine if there was any foul play."

"Oh, my God," Eleanor said, "you don't think—"

"Hold your horses," Robin interrupted. "Within a day or two, the cop got a DNA sample from Henry, which freaked him out."

Eleanor reached for Robin's hand. "You think Henry ran away because the police suspect that he pushed the Groves guy into Adrian's Abyss?"

Robin said she didn't know what to think, that Henry swore he quit chasing Groves after a few hundred yards. "But he told me that having punched Jordan and the link between him and his DNA will make him look guilty as hell, and then the whole sex thing will become public, and he couldn't bear it."

"Sad. So very, very sad," Julia said. "But I know Henry, and there's no way that kind man-child could kill anyone. No matter how mad he was."

"I'm with Julia," Eleanor said. "I think he'll come back to clear his name and make amends, for Hobey and Little Louis' sake . . . and yours."

"Oh, please, God, make my Babycakes be right," Robin said and began to cry. "I'd like that, like that more than you'll ever know. And, I'm with you, Julia, that darling man wouldn't harm a flea." She mixed a sniffle with a giggle. "A trout, maybe, but not a flea."

EIGHTEEN

W hen folks in the hamlet began to hunker down and get ready for a long, dark winter, as far as most were concerned, other than Julia's drawn-out battle with her "nasty" cancer, the McCutchen clan wasn't hitting any more bumps in the road than lots of other families. Few had given the Rajapakses' deer fence a second thought. And, because Frisky Forsythe was generally viewed as an unreliable gossip, Robin and Henry's salacious issue was nothing more than a rumor, although a juicy one. But, if it hadn't involved Big Louis' daughter, it wouldn't have raised one eyebrow.

The Jordan Groves case had long been forgotten until, on October 8, the *Lake Placid News* reported that the Essex County coroner had released the forensic autopsy results examining Groves' death. According to the newspaper,

THE CAUSE OF DEATH WAS STRAIGHTFORWARD: MR. GROVES DIED OF SEVERE HEAD INJURIES, RESULTING FROM A FALL OF APPROXI-MATELY 176 FEET INTO ADRIAN'S ABYSS. THE MANNER OF DEATH

The mention of a person of interest sent everyone in the Mc-Cutchen family into a tailspin, although all that any of them could pry out of the police was that two days after Henry had left Robin, he sold his Subaru Outback in Wilmington, North Carolina, for $11,000, cash. Other than that, he left not a trace. No rental car, no bus ticket, no plane ticket, no credit card charges, no phone calls. He'd pulled off what Robin called "a fucking Harry Houdini."

Like magic, Henry Honeywell had disappeared into thin air.

NINETEEN

The parking lot of the Tops Friendly Market in E-town (Elizabethtown to outsiders) is a big lot by Adirondack standards, even though it's really not very big, so it was no surprise that when Robin pulled in to do her weekly shopping, she found herself parked next to Frisky Forsythe, who was loading grocery bags into her car.

As Robin got out of her car, the two women almost collided, and Robin took a step back. "New car?"

"Why, yes," Frisky said. "I'm downsizing."

"Really?"

Frisky said, "Why, yes," again. "After you showed me that adorable two-bedroom up on Rocky Peak, I got to thinking that I'm too young and vibrant to live by myself, so I ditched the Mercedes, bought a Crosstrek, and I'm moving to The Cliffs."

"Young and vibrant?" Robin said. "I mean, come on, Frisky, The Cliffs isn't exactly populated by young and vibrant people. It's more like wrinkle city."

"Maybe, but there are some pretty juicy widowers there right now that might be looking for a little . . . who would know better than you, Robin . . . a little, shall we say, companionship?"

"*Chacun à son goût*," Robin said and turned to leave but stopped. "While we're talking about that adorable two-bedroom up on Rocky Peak, what exactly did you tell the police?"

"About the bungalow?"

"Don't play dumb with me, Frisky. It's not becoming. What did you tell the police about our phone call?"

"That you'd been visited by a man you called Jordan and that I heard Henry's voice."

"Did the police come to you, or couldn't you wait to spread one of your patented gossips?"

"Believe me, Robin, I never thought it would lead to this," Frisky said. "I simply thought it might help the police with their case."

"Well, I don't believe you, not for a minute," Robin said. "And if my dad ends up at The Cliffs, you'd better keep your horny little hands off of him. You've done enough damage to my family as it is."

"My, my, such righteous indignation. But have it your way, although I doubt many people will be sympathetic toward you when all your dirty laundry becomes public."

"Dirty laundry? What are you talking about?"

Frisky finished loading her groceries and climbed into her new Subaru. Before she shut the door, she smiled and gave Robin a short wave. "You know damn well what I'm talking about. And Sgt. Oswald does, too."

Robin leaned against her car as Frisky drove away. She covered her face with her hands and began to sob. At this moment, she didn't care if anyone was watching. She thought the damage had already been done and wondered, *What have I done? What has Henry done? How can I make it all go away?*

TWENTY

The afternoon before Julia's surgery, with Ravi, Robin, and Eleanor—even Father Quinlan—huddled at her bedside, and swarms of doctors, technologists, and nurses attending to her, Julia had never felt more alone. When she struggled to control her anger and fear and find an answer to why she'd been singled out, she realized that cancer didn't care who or what you are, that it was nothing more than a random piece of maliciousness. And, when Father Quinlan encouraged her to place her faith in God, Julia confessed that she was a believer in her own way, but in what she didn't really know, perhaps a greater being, certainly something bigger than she could imagine.

Later, when she and Ravi were finally alone, Julia admitted that she was struggling to let go of all her uncertainties and turn herself over to her oncologist and her surgeon. She said she was trying hard to put herself in their hands no matter what her odds were, no matter the outcome. "It makes no difference," she said, "without them, I have no chance at all."

"You've got every chance in the world, and now it's time for you to get some sleep," Ravi said.

Julia took his hand, squeezed it tightly, and smiled up at him. "Do me a hugie?"

Ravi said of course, anything, anything at all.

"Will you put an easement on our little piece of heaven? Like we promised Dad we would."

"Of course, but why now?"

"Call it unfinished business, if you will, or just tidying up, but it would put my mind at ease in case I don't make it through all this."

Ravi kept hold of her hand. "I'll do it ASAP. But no worries, you'll make it through tomorrow."

"I'm not talking about the operation," Julia said and began to sob. "I'm talking about the whole, ugly process. I don't want Dad to remember me as someone who couldn't keep her word; who cared more about money than protecting our beloved Adirondacks." She freed her hand from Ravi's and wiped at her tears. "And cancel the fence, too. Will you? Right now, our lives are complicated enough without worrying about deer and mice."

"And alligators?" Ravi asked.

"And alligators," Julia said. "God, Ravi, but I love you."

"Love you, too," Ravi said and kissed her. Not a goodnight kiss, but a kiss intended to offer love, hope, and reassurance. "Now get some rest. Tomorrow we begin the battle. Together, every step of the way. Bird by bird."

And, so, the next day, Julia's colorectal surgeon, with assistance from a da Vinci Robot, became her God.

Before all this ugly cancer business with Julia started, Ravi was an enigma to lots of folks in the hamlet. Most viewed him as an aloof ne'er-do-well foreigner, a wealthy elitist who couldn't find a comfortable way to fit into the local community. But the minute Ravi learned of Julia's illness, he emerged from his Barcalounger, seemingly having found a meaningful use for his many millions and idle time. It's safe to say that nothing escaped him, that he was always one step ahead of everyone when it came to making sure that Julia had the best and most loving care. And, rather quickly, he gained the respect of all who came in contact with him.

Mid-December, while she was still repulsed by the sight of her stoma, the bulbous, gooey donut of intestine that protruded on her belly, Julia's chemo regimen began in an outpatient clinic where every other Monday she was hooked up to an IV bag labeled ATTENTION HAZARDOUS MATERIAL. After the second cycle of treatment she had lost eight pounds, and everything that she was warned could happen, did happen. Her face became a sickly gray. Handfuls of hair came out in her comb. Food began to have a metallic taste, and she lost her appetite. Most nights she threw up, usually more than once. And, she spent her days in a sleepy, chemo fog, doubled over with cramps and diarrhea.

With nine more chemo sessions yet to come, Julia wondered when her nightmare would end and if she had the strength to soldier on. But, in the end, she gave in to the toxic ravaging of her body and accepted whatever happened as inevitable. Always cold, she wrapped herself in a blanket. Her body was almost hairless, and she wore a wig to hide the fact that her trademark, her thick, blonde ponytail, was no more. Nose bleeds, sores in her mouth, and chemo burns on her skin were common occurrences. She slept ten to twelve hours a night, curled in the fetal position. Too nauseous to read or watch TV, let alone eat, she lost track of time. Ravi tried to keep her hopeful and read her the many cards and letters from well-wishers and snippets from the newspaper, but many days Julia didn't even acknowledge his presence.

TWENTY-ONE

As always, the windscreen was down and the Llewellins were huddled on the back seat as Big Louis parked his olive drab Jeep in the circle of Robin's drive. He raised a hand and told the dogs to stay when Robin appeared at the front door. She considered saying, "To what do I owe this honor?" but, instead, she simply invited her father to come into the house.

Big Louis stepped in front of a shattered headlight and dented fender and said, "That won't be necessary. This is a business call."

Robin asked if he wanted to chat about the Home Owners Association, then added, "What happened to your jeep?"

Big Louis said nothing had happened.

Robin asked if he dinged it driving at night.

Her father told her that it was none of her damn business.

"Okay," Robin said, "Then let me try this one on for size: great news about Julia's fence, huh?"

Big Louis gave her a blank look. "Enough of that. What I want to know is why the three of you want to lock me up in a home;

why you want to get me out of your way, like I'm a burden to you."

Robin flushed. "Dad, for God's sake, no one's trying to get rid of you. We're just trying to make sure that someone's nearby in case you need help. You'll have to admit that you're getting a little bit too old to live all by yourself. You're no spring chicken. Yes? No?"

"Maybe. Maybe not. But not right now."

"But when, Dad? Are you going to wait until you have a real problem? Until it's too late?"

Big Louis turned and climbed back into his Jeep. "It's none of your damn business, but when I do, I'll come live with you. There. That make you happy?"

"Don't plan on it," Robin said, "because it isn't going to happen. My husband's disappeared, and I just damn well may sell this place and move back to Boston to be closer to my boys."

"And leave me high and dry?" Big Louis asked.

"Isn't that the way you want it?"

Big Louis slammed the Jeep into gear. "To hell with you. To hell with all three of you."

As he drove around the circle and out the dirt drive, Robin pulled her well-manicured hands from her blue jeans' pockets and silently, but enthusiastically, gave her father the bird.

Once home, Big Louis pulled on his blaze orange vest and cap and lifted his beloved Winchester 21 from the pegs by the front door. He turned the shotgun in his hands to admire it and thought, *try as they might, they can't stop me from being who I am.* Once outside, he paused for a moment to study the sky above the great range. *Looks and smells like rain.* He shrugged. He thought he'd have time enough to get a shot or two at a ruffed grouse before it was too dark.

As he approached the kennels, the Llewellins sat, sweeping their tails over the concrete floor, waiting for their master to release them. "You're the only friends I've got," he said. "First, Owen turns against me and then Eleanor. And now, Robin. The whole world's gone to hell in a handbasket." He unlatched the kennel gate, released Tray, and thought, *what the hell, this one's more for us than the birds,* and let the elderly Sweetheart and the puppy Blanche join in the hunt.

He opened his shotgun, dropped a shell in both chambers, and picked his way along the western ridge of Bobcat Mountain, the fire tower on the mountain's summit appearing and disappearing as heavy gray clouds swept over it. Rain began to fall, lightly at first. Big Louis thought that the storm was a blessing in contrast to the harshness of his daughters' behavior. He shook his head in disgust. *It isn't possible to do enough for them, to ever satisfy them. Good God, what do they think I am? A bottomless money pit? Or just some feeble old man who has become easy prey?*

He hunted slowly, the dense cover muted by the darkening sky. Sweetheart stayed at heel while Blanche stopped to smell everything she came across. Suddenly, Tray began to make game, his nose inches above the ground, his body tensed, his whole being locked on a scent. Big Louis snapped the Winchester shut and urged his setter to find the bird.

Tray hunted in a circle. Big Louis stood still waiting for him to freeze, his feathery tail straight as an arrow, his foreleg tucked, and his nose pointing his quarry. Instead, there was a heavy crashing sound and a dark form burst from the cover and shinnied up a nearby hemlock, stopping at the first set of branches just above Big Louis' head. "Well, I'll be goddamned, Tray," he said. "Treeing a bear? Now, that's a first."

The bear climbed to higher branches and stared down at them. After a moment, Tray lost interest and went back to hunting, with Big Louis trudging behind him. The rain began to fall more heavily, trickling down the back of Big Louis' collar and dripping from the bill of his cap while thunder rolled along the great range. *Adirondack weather. The temperature must have dropped twenty degrees since I left the house.*

Big Louis stumbled, climbing over a small blowdown, regained his balance, and strained to locate Tray. Lightning illuminated the skyline above Mount Marcy and he caught a glimpse of the setter hunting to his left. As they approached a thicket that had produced many flushes in the past, Tray froze, but instead of going on point, drew his tail between his legs, raised his hackles, and uttered a long, low growl. It was a behavior Big Louis had never seen before, and he wondered what the hell was going on. He took a few steps to see what was bothering the setter when a gentle voice said, "Louis, dear, you should get in out of the rain. You'll catch your death of cold."

"Katherine?"

"Why, of course."

Big Louis squinted to see his wife more clearly. She seemed so young and healthy, the way he always remembered her. "You look well. Beautiful as ever," he said and reached for her hands, but she held them close behind her back. He was at a loss for words and leaned down to stroke Sweetheart's ears as she pressed against his leg. Thunder crashed directly overhead, and Big Louis straightened, bracing for the lighting that drilled through the darkness no more than a hundred yards away. He hesitated, then asked, "What brings you here?"

"You needed someone to talk to."

"As always, you're so right. For years our girls told me that I was everything, but now they don't give a damn about what I think or feel. I've lost their respect, Katherine, and there's no way to get it back. No possible way, so what's the sense of going on? I'm nothing more than a vacant shell. It's no wonder they can't wait to see me locked up somewhere."

"No dear, not locked up; looked after as you grow older. They think that's what's best for you."

"Or they simply want me out of the way."

Katherine's image became absorbed by its surroundings and Big Louis wiped rain from his eyes and took a step closer to see her better. "No, no," he said. "Don't go. I need your help. You know I treated them fair and square, don't you? Please say yes."

"Oh, my, Louis, you're so black and white. Still no grays on your palette. That's one of parenting's great dilemmas. Yield to them. Tell Eleanor how much you love her. Be gentle with Robin, for she's a ship without a rudder right now. Most of all, be kind to Julia. Soon she will need all the love you can give her. If you don't, you'll be filled with regrets."

"Regrets?"

"Yes, my dear man, regrets. She won't be with you much longer."

"Oh, my God. Katherine. Oh, my God," Big Louis said. "But they're driving me crazy. And all I wanted was what was best for them."

"The girls' needs are varied, and they've changed, as have their relationships. So, yield to their desires and ask forgiveness from each. You need to love and respect them as much as you want them to love and respect you."

Once more, the image began to fade. "No, Katherine," Big Louis said. "Please don't leave me. Tell me that you know I'm sorry. Tell me it wasn't my fault."

"Don't fret, dear Louis. I don't blame you and will never leave you. Farewell until we meet again."

"God damn it, Katherine, take me with you. There's nothing left here for me. Nothing. I don't want to go on like this, please, let me join you. I'm so goddamned sorry."

For a moment, Big Louis stood frozen in place. His pleas were drowned out by the wind-driven rain and rolling thunder that was trapped within the walls of the great range. Slowly he shifted his hands to the barrels of his shotgun and swung it like an ax at a nearby hemlock, splintering the stock. He yelled and struck the tree over and over until he had expended all of his anger and threw what was left of the gun into the heavy cover. "No more," he said and pulled off his cap and vest and threw them into the woods as well. "Done. Big Louis McCutchen is done." He whistled the dogs to his side and commanded, "Home."

He walked slowly, careful not to catch one of his boots in the undergrowth, his chamois shirt soaking wet and heavy. In the distance he could make out the silhouette of a small building. A few more steps and two figures, and the beam of a flashlight, approached him. A woman's voice called to him. "Is that you, Dad?"

"Yes, it's me. I'm here with your mother."

"That's great, Dad, just great. It's your daughter, Eleanor. Your friend Owen is with me, too."

"Eleanor? What the hell are you doing out on a night like this?"

"Looking for you. Let's get you in the shack and out of this rain. You'll catch your death of cold."

Owen lit the propane lantern in the sugar shack where he and Big Louis had boiled a small batch of maple syrup every spring for as long as Owen could remember. He set a fire in the woodstove and handed Big Louis a black and white checked work shirt that hung by the door. "One of yours," he said. "Put it on, and let's get you warmed up."

Big Louis changed from his sodden shirt and collapsed in a rickety wood chair close to the stove. He studied the dogs as they huddled close to him and asked Owen if he had any daughters. When Owen reminded him that he and Donna had never had any children, Big Louis said, "Well, you're damn lucky you didn't." He looked at Eleanor. "Wouldn't you agree?"

"You're asking me? Dad, I'm Eleanor. Your youngest daughter. Remember? And, of course, I don't agree; you'd be lost without us."

Big Louis crossed his arms across his chest to warm himself and sat silently, mesmerized by the flames dancing in the woodstove. "I guess you're right. I'm a bit confused." He looked up at Eleanor. "Any news on your sister?"

"Julia?"

"Yes. Lovely Julia."

"She's asked Ravi to ease her property and not build the fence if that's what you mean."

Big Louis asked, very quietly, "What's gotten into her?"

"I'm afraid she's tidying up things because she's near the end."

Her father moved the toe of his boot back and forth over Sweetheart, who slept curled at his feet. "Why should any of us survive—dogs, you, me—when your mother was killed for no good reason, and Julia's so damn sick? It's just not fair. It's not fair to them or us."

"Tell Julia you feel that way," Eleanor said. "Tell her how much you love her."

"That's what your mother said. She said I should tell you, too." He nodded a few times, and his chin dropped to his chest.

Eleanor started to say something, but Owen raised a finger to his lips and whispered, "Let him sleep. It's been a rough day for him. And you too. We can talk about all this tomorrow."

The latch on the crude wood door to the sugar shack rattled with the wind, and the rain tattooed the tin roof as Eleanor reached to squeeze Owen's hand. Her eyes, like those of her father's great friend, were filled with tears.

TWENTY-TWO

Little Louis and his younger brother Hobey came home from boarding school for the Christmas holidays. It was the first time the boys had been in the valley since their father had disappeared, and they brought a renewed energy to Robin's solitary existence. They also brought her what they thought would be a special Christmas present. Inside an envelope containing a letter from their father postmarked December 3rd, Key West, Florida, a small, blue envelope was addressed to their mother. The note inside, written on a brown Starbucks paper napkin, read: I'm trying to heal. Goldilocks is fine. Merry Christmas.

Robin didn't know if she should laugh or cry, but in the end, she accepted the note for what it was, a reassurance that her beloved Goldilocks and her Honeybunch were alive and well.

For Julia, Christmas and the ushering in of 2016 passed without her noticing.

Eleanor's holidays weren't much of a break, either. Thanks to all the snow, and rain, and ice, then more snow, rain, and ice, and the windchill factor on Whiteface occasionally dropping to

35° below zero, her outings on cross-country skis or snowshoes were replaced by strapping crampons on her boots just to walk to her car. Her high point was cooking Christmas dinner for her nieces and nephews and Robin at Big Louis' house; the downside was that Julia wasn't well enough to attend, and Ravi elected not to leave her on what he worried might be her last Christmas.

As far as Big Louis was concerned, his inability to remember some of his grandchildren's names and his repeated proclaiming that someone had stolen his beloved Winchester became "the new normal" within his family.

TWENTY-THREE

Small puddles of water dotted Robin's soggy lawn while thinning patches of snow lingered in the shadows surrounding her property. She stood with Owen at the edge of her driveway, shifting from one L.L. Bean-booted-foot to the other while cradling a large FOR SALE sign. Without Henry to turn to, she'd asked Owen to help her put up the sign, one of the many things that made her realize how much she'd relied on Henry and how difficult it was being a single woman. And, yes, how much she missed and loved her Honeybunch.

As though he was making a mental note, Owen said, "Too damn warm for February. It's going to screw up the sugaring." He set a sledgehammer on its head by his feet and turned to Robin. "Well, young lady, you sure you want to do this? You don't have to, you know."

"Oh, but I do, Owen. I do. Levi Lamb's just too small for me, given what I've done."

"Water over the dam," Owen said. "People are far more concerned with this crappy weather and their own problems than one nasty rumor. I think I know what people talk about, and if it's anything about your family, it's about your sister's health."

"You're sweet, Owen. You really are. But I haven't had one call from someone who's looking for a house since. . . since the incident. Not one. No one wants to do business with me anymore. Besides, I'm so embarrassed by what I did and Henry's disappearing that I need to get out of Dodge. Simple as that. So, I'm going back to Boston to be close to the boys. Where I still have some friends. Where I can start over."

Owen rested a hand on Robin's shoulder. "And while you're waiting to sell your house, what are you going to do? You've always said that this is a two-to-three-year market."

"Good, God, Owen, I didn't call you up here for a therapy session. Let's just plant this fucking sign where people can see it and get on with it." She placed the sign close to her driveway and smiled up at him. "Don't worry. I'll make the best of my time." She laughed. "Maybe I'll spend it looking after His Bigness."

Owen turned and looked down the road. "Well, speaking of the devil, look who's coming."

"On, shit," Robin said.

"I'll second that," Owen said.

They watched as Big Louis parked his Jeep but didn't move; he just held onto the steering wheel and yelled, "You've got to help me. Please. Help me."

Owen hurried toward him. "What's up?"

Big Louis climbed from his Jeep and muttered, "Sweetheart's gone."

"What do you mean she's gone?" Owen asked. "She run away?"

Big Louis dropped to his knees, but Owen caught him before he fell face-down on the muddy lawn. "No. She's gone, Owen. I went out to the kennel this morning and she was dead. Stiff as a board. My dear old Sweetheart."

Robin rushed to her father and wrapped her arms around him. "Oh, Dad. I'm so sorry. So, so sorry. She was such a lovely old girl." She looked at Owen. "Change of plans. We can do this sign thing some other time. I'll take Dad home to say a proper goodbye to Sweetheart if you can take her to the vet's when we're through."

"Sounds like a plan," Owen said. He helped Big Louis to his feet, steadied him, and guided him to the passenger's seat of the Jeep. As Robin climbed in and struggled to jam the Jeep into gear, Owen gave her a knowing smile. "There may be more for you to do here than I thought."

The following morning, Robin and Owen stood where they'd been standing when Big Louis had interrupted them. Once again, Robin held the FOR SALE sign while Owen hefted the sledgehammer.

"You still want to go through with this?" Owen asked.

"What is this, twenty questions?"

"No, but just one more?"

"Okay," Robin said. "But only one."

Owen asked if she was going to put a conservation easement on her property before she sold it.

"A fair question, but the answer is no. I don't have the foggiest where things are going to lead with Henry, and I'd be foolish not to get as much for the house as I can, just in case I get the fuzzy end of the financial lollipop."

"Even though a conservation easement is what you agreed to when your father gave you the land, and both your sisters have eased theirs?"

"Their situations are a lot different than mine." She steadied the sign where she wanted it and nodded. "Maybe, if things change for me, who knows? But now, as Henry would say, it's time to fish or cut bait."

Two dark, dreary months passed without anyone showing the slightest interest in buying Robin's house. "Maybe it's because of all the snow and ice," she told Eleanor, "but no one has given me a call, no one, not even a fucking curiosity seeker."

As a result, Robin formulated a personal recovery plan. She began to visit town more frequently than she had in the past as though she was campaigning for mayor, trying to be accepted as a member of the community once again. And, she was seeking forgiveness, for what she wasn't quite sure. She "chatted up" everyone she ran into and regularly attended the Sunday service at Stuart Quinlan's church. She even convened a three-day off-site retreat for the board of the LLHA to revisit their mission and update their plans for the future.

And, once a week, without fail, she wrote Little Louis and Hobey, trying to buoy their spirits and catch up on their news because she had so little to report on her end. She ended every letter with, "Still no word here from Dad. What about you?"

TWENTY-FOUR

Heavy rainstorms in early April ushered in the mud season and flooded the valley. As a result, many dirt roads became too "greasy" to navigate. It was during this bleak stretch that Julia's oncologist called Ravi to say that they had some major decisions to make and that she'd like to meet with him as soon as possible.

That afternoon, Ravi, accompanied by Sandy Janeway, met with Dr. Ritter in a sparsely decorated conference room at the UVM Cancer Center. Once Dr. Ritter had ordered the papers in front of her, she looked up at Ravi. "I'm sure you sense that the news isn't good."

Ravi drew an audible breath and placed both hands over his mouth.

Sandy Janeway shifted in his chair and rested a hand on Ravi's shoulder.

"The bottom line is the chemo hasn't accomplished what we'd hoped it would. Quite the opposite. Julia has become jaundiced, and a CT scan shows a recurrent tumor in her pelvis and that her cancer has metastasized to her lungs, liver and bones. Moreover, the neuropathy in her fingers and toes is so severe that if her chemo isn't terminated, we fear she won't regain the use of her hands and feet."

Ravi leaned toward Dr. Ritter. "What you're telling me is that Julia's not going to make it."

"Certainly not on this therapeutic path, but there's at least one clinical trial we could enroll her in."

Dr. Janeway asked, "And if you did enroll her, might the experimental drugs cure Julia or simply extend her life?"

"Impossible to say at this point. Their efficacy has yet to be confirmed."

"That another way of saying they're long shots?" Ravi asked.

"Depends on your point of view," Dr. Ritter said. "Researchers refer to them as compounds which show early promise. As for the long term, it's anybody's guess."

"A word, here, Dr. Ritter?" Sandy Janeway asked.

"Of course."

Sandy turned to Ravi. "This is the medical crossroads for all of us, doctors, patients, families, but especially for physicians like Dr. Ritter who deal with this type of situation far more than they'd like. For me, nothing more than a country GP but your old family friend, at this point I think the best thing you can do for Julia is to stop her chemotherapy, make her as comfortable as possible at home, surround her with family and let her know how much you all love her. I think it would be futile, almost cruel, to put her through any more treatment. Just one man's opinion, but I don't come by it easily."

Ravi asked if Dr. Ritter agreed with Dr. Janeway.

She nodded. "It's time for hospice."

"Is Julia aware of this?" Ravi asked.

"No. Not yet. I wanted to talk with you first, but I'm sure she senses it," Dr. Ritter said.

"I need some time to think . . . or something," Ravi said, fighting to hold back his tears. "We're only just beginning . . . and the little ones . . ."

When Ravi was sure that the kids were asleep, he sat beside Julia on their bed and reached for her hand. "How are you feeling?"

She struggled to keep her eyes open and forced a smile. "The same. I'm nauseous and exhausted. This wasn't worth it."

"Wasn't worth what?"

"Feeling awful for all this time for nothing."

"For nothing?"

"You're super cute, but yes, for nothing. Dr. Ritter threw the kitchen sink at me and it didn't work."

"Who says?" Ravi asked.

"I do. I'm dying. You know it, and I know it. And it's okay. I've been preparing myself ever since all this began."

"We could try some experimental drugs. That might help."

"No, Ravi. None of that. No more drugs. Keep the kids close and never leave my side, and I'll be fine."

"You sure?"

"I'm positive, and right now, I'd like to go to sleep. We can talk with the kids in the morning." She smiled for a second, and her eyes closed. "Love you."

Ravi shook his head and looked away. "Love you, too. Always will. Always."

TWENTY-FIVE

Robin wrapped and unwrapped the phone cord around her fingers while waiting for Eleanor to answer her call. When Eleanor picked up, Robin said, "Where have you been, Babycakes? I've been trying to reach you for hours."

Eleanor said that she'd paid a quick call on Julia and then holed up to let her hair down with April and tell her how depressing her life was. And do a little meditating. And a little praying. "But enough about me. It's just that Julia's situation is the saddest thing I've ever experienced. She's at peace and worries about everyone but herself." She hesitated. "She's the best of us."

"Absolutely. But that doesn't mean the two of us can't do better. We owe it to her."

"Wow, big sister. Listen to you," Eleanor said. "What's come over you?"

"Nothing and everything. Maybe it's as simple as Henry leaving me. Whatever, it's time I stopped being such a control freak, such a judgmental bitch. But that's not why I called. I was on my way out to visit Julia when Sgt. Oswald called—"

"With news about Henry?" Eleanor interrupted.

"Don't I wish. But not even close. You sitting down?"

"Oh, God, what is it?"

"You're not going to believe it. Around eight this morning, the police answered a 911. The caller said that Dad was dragging himself down his driveway, calling for Owen."

Eleanor asked if this was some kind of a sick joke.

"No such luck, Babycakes. And, you ready for this?" Robin didn't wait for Eleanor to answer. "He was stark naked and suffering from hypothermia."

"Oh, sweet Jesus."

"He'd better be sweet," Robin said. "We're going to need all the help we can get. It's like Dad was following our script. He fell in the shower and broke his hip. Owen and I are with him now at the Medical Center in Saranac Lake."

Eleanor asked why he didn't call one of them.

"He says he couldn't find the phone, and we never answer when he calls, anyway, so, he thought he'd take the matter into his own hands, the way he always has."

"Lovely. Just lovely," Eleanor said.

"You got it. Big Louis being Big Louis. But he knows that they're going to operate on him tomorrow and give him a new hip, and that's fine by him. Considering the early morning nightmare, all's now pretty much on an even keel. He's warmed up and seems to be comfortable, and he's been assured he can watch the Red Sox games on the TV in his room. The only thing that agitated him is who will look after the dogs, but Owen says he'll take care of them.

"Owen being Owen, but I'll do it. The Llewellins are a family matter," Eleanor said. "And I'll go to the hospital tonight to check on him."

"Babycakes, you're the best."

"I'm trying."

"Me, too. See you tonight," Robin said, then added, "Love you, Babycakes. Love you a lot."

"Love you, too," Eleanor said and headed up the mountain to look after Big Louis' beloved Blanche and Tray.

TWENTY-SIX

Ravi met his father-in-law outside the Adirondack Medical Center and carefully loaded him and his walker into Julia's SUV. Once buckled up, Ravi asked, "How do you feel? It sounds like the operation was a great success." Big Louis didn't seem to hear him or elected not to answer. After a moment, Ravi tried again. "All set, sir?"

Big Louis asked where they were headed.

"My house first, so you can pay a call on Julia, then I'll take you home."

"Can't that wait?" Big Louis asked. "I just broke my hip, you know."

"I appreciate that, but Julia's taken a turn for the worse, and I think it's important that you see her today. What's more, she's really looking forward to seeing you."

Big Louis began nodding and dozed off, and Ravi drove to the Lake Placid by-pass before his father-in-law stirred. "Still a bit drowsy from the anesthesia, Mr. McCutchen?"

Big Louis shrugged. "I'd like to go home and go to bed."

"I understand, sir. The visit with Julia will be short. I can promise you that. Having visitors is a lot of work for her right now."

"Why can't it wait? I just broke my hip, you know."

"I understand, Mr. McCutchen, but it can't wait."

"And why is that?"

Ravi stared straight ahead. "Julia's dying, and her doctor says she doesn't have much time left."

"The doctors couldn't save Katherine either, you know. I don't have much time for any of them. You can't be sure they're right, so I'd like to go home."

Ravi passed the Olympic ski jumping complex and drove without speaking for a few more moments. Finally, he pulled into a lookout for Cascade Lake and, keeping both hands on the steering wheel, turned to face Big Louis. "I know you've been through a lot with your surgery, but, for a change, Mr. McCutchen, this isn't about you. This is about your daughter, Julia. So, right now, there's nothing more important to me or your family than Julia. Nothing."

Big Louis slapped his hands on the dash. "You can't talk to me that way. I'm your father-in-law, for God's sake."

"I don't mean to be disrespectful, sir. I'm just trying to have you register that Julia's dying, that you're about to lose one of your daughters, and I'm about to lose my wife, and my children are about to lose their mother. Got it?"

Big Louis didn't speak. He folded his hands in his lap and stared at the ranks of leafless, ghostly-white paper birches that bordered the narrow lake.

"God damn it, Mr. McCutchen, answer me," Ravi said. "Do you get it or not?"

Big Louis looked at Ravi, his blue eyes bright with tears. "I'm sorry. I had no idea."

"Thank you, sir. I'm having trouble believing it, too," Ravi said and pulled onto the road south.

Big Louis sat quietly, occasionally wringing his hands. As they approached the turn-off for Levi Lamb, he said, "A favor?"

"Certainly, sir. Anything. Anything at all."

He asked if Ravi had a razor that he could borrow. He said he'd like to look presentable before Julia saw him.

Big Louis positioned his walker close to Julia's bed and reached to touch her shoulder to wake her. He gave Ravi a worried look when she didn't respond and asked if they were too late.

Ravi shook his head. "No. It's okay. Take your time."

Big Louis gently squeezed Julia's shoulder and said quietly, "Sweetheart, it's me. Your dad."

Julia's eyes opened, and a smile crossed her face. Slowly, with several pauses, she asked, "To what do I owe this honor?"

Her father gave out a guttural, animal-like sound and began to sob.

Ravi wrapped his arms around his father-in-law from behind to steady him. Big Louis covered Ravi's hands with his large, knobby-knuckled hands and asked, "Are you feeling okay?"

"No. I feel rotten," Julia said.

"I'll bet," Big Louis said. "Is there anything I can do?"

"You being here is all I need."

Big Louis wiped at his tears. "You mean it?"

Julia reached to touch him. "Of course, I mean it."

"Oh, thank God," Big Louis said. "But how in the hell do I kiss you?"

"Just a second, sir," Ravi said. He gestured to the hospice nurse and together they lifted Julia's frail body toward her father.

Big Louis took her face in his hands. "I love you so much. You're my gentle little girl." For a moment, he held his lips against her cheek, his tears mixing with hers, and told her again how very much he loved her.

"Love you, too, Dad," Julia said. She drew a few labored breaths. "The circle's now complete."

Ravi and the nurse carefully lowered Julia back in the bed, and Ravi nodded at his father-in-law. "I think your gentle little girl would like to take a nap now. I guess it's time to say goodbye."

"I can't. Don't have the courage. Just can't face it," Big Louis said and turned his walker and shuffled toward the bedroom door.

Once back in the SUV, Big Louis asked where they were going. "To Eleanor's," Ravi said. "I'll bet that sounds pretty good after all you've been through."

"Will you be there?"

"No, but Eleanor will. You're going to stay with her until you're back on your feet."

"But, you won't be there?"

"No." Ravi laughed. "I can't tell if you're disappointed or relieved."

"You'll be looking after Julia. Right?"

"Right."

"And Eleanor will look after the Llewellins and me. Right?"

Ravi said, "Right, again."

For the first time since Ravi could remember, his father-in-law called him by name and smiled at him. "Well, Ravi, I'll miss you, but Julia needs you more than I do."

The day after Big Louis' visit, the hospice nurse told Ravi that she didn't think Julia would make it through the night and suggested that her sisters and the children be with her as much as possible from here on out. Well past the kids' usual bedtime, Julia became agitated and tried to rip free from her colostomy bag. The children were encouraged to tell her how much they loved her and kiss her good night before Eleanor ushered them off to bed.

At approximately two in the morning, with Ravi holding her hand and Robin and Eleanor standing at her bedside, smiling and crying, quietly reminiscing about their childhoods, Julia succumbed to her long, exhausting battle with cancer.

She was thirty-eight years old.

TWENTY-SEVEN

The memorial service for Julia was held at All Saints Episcopal Church on the last Friday in April. Along with Ravi's parents and his sister from Sri Lanka, the McCutchen family and a large crowd of townsfolk filled the church and spilled out onto the lawn. The only family member missing was Henry Honeywell, who no one knew how to reach, including the State Police.

Eleanor read the familiar selection from John that assures us that there are many mansions in God's house. Little Louis, the president of his class at Groton like his grandfather many years before him, led the psalm recitation that comforts us that the Lord will preserve our souls. Father Quinlan delivered the eulogy, and Sandy Janeway shared several humorous remembrances.

It was Robin's tribute that folks in the valley remembered most. Dressed in a black pants suit and patent leather heels, she herded the Rajapakse children and Jeter to the lectern. Once the kids were carefully arranged and Jeter lay at their feet, all joined hands, and Robin thanked everyone for celebrating the life of their most gentle, loving family member.

"Kasun, Hansi and Sarah have asked me to share with you what they think their mother would have liked to have heard and what they'd like you to hear. But first, I have to explain that this is their nightly ritual, Julia's way of having her kids believe in something unimaginable, something that's filled with goodness and love. Like her, I would add something that encourages them to be kind to others and themselves. It starts with what Julia called a loving-kindness prayer or, in the kids' shorthand, an 'LKP' and ends with three essential prayers. It's a ritual that all three of these adorable kids promised Julia they would continue for the rest of their lives. So, we're keeping that promise here this morning."

Robin let go of the children's hands, smoothed a crumpled piece of paper on the lectern, and looked down at the children. "Okay? Still good?"

Kasun and Hansi nodded, and Sara again reached for her hand. A smile crossed Robin's face, but her eyes glistened with tears. "Phew. They're unbelievable."

She paused, then began reading from the paper. "Here's Hansi's LKP: 'May I see the good in people and always smile the way my mom does.' And Kasun prays: 'May I comfort Dad because I know how much he misses and loves Mom and how much she loves him." Robin fought back her tears. "And Sara prays that she may be as kind to animals as her mommy. So, there you have three loving-kindness prayers that kind of wrap my sister up in a nutshell from those who knew her the best."

Again, Robin leaned down to the children and whispered, "I think we're doing great." She straightened and wiped tears from her cheeks. "Every night, Julia ended with a prayer for help, or with a thank you, or a 'wow,' a comment on an outstanding accomplishment, like Kasun's 'wow' to me for finally seeing a Bicknell's Thrush." Robin shook her head. "Sorry. I just had to get that in." The church filled with laughter, her comment offering a break from the pain everyone shared with Julia's children.

Robin drew a deep breath. "Kasun and Hansi and Sara chose to combine all three essential prayers into one with the hope that it would make their mommy happy." She looked toward Stuart Quinlan and said, "If this doesn't do the trick, God only knows what will."

More laughter from the congregation and a broad smile from the reverend.

"Well, here goes," Robin said. "My dad and Ravi and Eleanor and I, and all of us I'm sure, along with Julia's children, offer the following prayer: We pray for help to be strong in Julia's absence and carry out our lives in the kind and loving manner that would make her proud of us. We give thanks to Julia for her abundant love for each of us and for her teaching us to love ourselves. And we offer a great big 'wow!' for Julia being the best mom, sister, daughter and wife the world has ever known."

At the reception in the parish hall, the mourners inched their way from family member to family member to express their love and sorrow. All wanted to tell Robin how much they enjoyed the way she represented the children, many implying that she was once again welcome in the community. Finally, they moved on to Big Louis, whose massive frame looked oddly out of place as he sat in a small blue plastic chair with Eleanor at his side, frequently stroking his back to comfort him and keep him focused. He seemed bewildered by the condolences of so many townspeople whose names he couldn't recall. What seemed to confuse him at one minute and buoy his spirits the next was the outpouring of admiration and respect for all he'd done for the community.

But, it was Frisky Forsythe's greeting him with a kiss on the lips and saying that he'd be given the very best of care if he decided to move into The Cliffs that triggered Big Louis to tell Eleanor that he'd heard enough of this nonsense, that he wanted to get the hell out of here, go home and take a nap.

Eleanor agreed that the time had come and signaled to Owen that she needed help loading her father into the car and asked if he'd follow her home. Once underway, she said, "Sad, huh, Dad? I mean really, really sad."

"Your mother's death was sadder."

Eleanor grimaced as she turned onto the narrow dirt road that led to her house. "Dad, you can't compare the two. That doesn't afford either the importance it deserves. Both are the saddest things *ever* for me."

"To each his own," Big Louis said.

Eleanor started to say something but thought better of it and drove the rest of the way without speaking. As she parked, her father's chin dropped to his chest, and she could hear the heavy breathing of his sleep. She quietly unlatched his seat belt, pulled his walker from the back seat, and gently shook his shoulder. "Time to rise and shine." Big Louis woke with a grunt and looked at her as though he wasn't sure where he was or who she was. "It's okay, Dad, you're at my house," Eleanor said. "Now, remember what they taught you at the hospital: swing both feet out, nice and easy, and push yourself up from the seat and the console."

Big Louis surprised her by doing what he was told. Once free of the car, he struggled to gain his balance. Eleanor offered her hands to steady him as he lurched forward, all 6'5", 260 pounds of him knocking her to the ground as he fell.

Eleanor sprang to her feet. "Good God, Dad, are you alright? Did you hurt your hip?"

Big Louis lay face down. He didn't move and didn't speak.

Again she asked if he'd hurt his hip.

Her father lifted his head to look at her. "I'm okay, God damn it. My hip's okay." He pushed his upper body off the ground and lay back down. "But I can't get up. Don't just stand there; help me."

Eleanor told him not to move, that Owen would be there in a minute.

Big Louis asked what the hell was keeping him when Owen pulled into the drive, rushed to him and helped him to his feet, and set his walker in front of him. "Okay, boss, there you go," he said. " How's your hip?"

"What's with all of you? I told you, my hip's fine."

Eleanor waved a silencing hand at Owen. "Great, Dad, just great. Now, how about a little lunch and then a nap?"

"No lunch," Big Louis said and pointed at Owen. "And get him out of here. I want to be alone. You're all too damn much for me."

TWENTY-EIGHT

A week after Julia's service, Robin and Ravi arrived in Eleanor's kitchen as Big Louis was finishing his daily bowl of Wheaties. Eleanor suggested that Ravi help her father move to the living room to get things underway. Once Big Louis had settled in his favorite spot on her couch, she called from the kitchen, asking if she could bring him a cup of coffee.

"With cream but no sugar," Big Louis said.

"Coming right up." Eleanor looked at Robin. "How in the world could I have forgotten that?"

"A killer of a question," Robin said. "But, don't forget, Babycakes: *Unus pro omnibus, omnes pro uno.*"

Eleanor laughed. "Does that mean Ravi's now one of the three musketeers?"

"For certain. He's one of the sweetest men on the planet."

"Wow, that's a change of tune."

Robin smiled. "That's life in the fast lane, Babycakes. Life in the fast lane. He's so gentle and understanding with those kids; it's a wonder he survived the Wall Street jungle."

"Julia saw his kindness early on, way before the rest of us."

"Like she did with so many other things," Robin said. "God, but I miss her."

"Me, too," Eleanor said and hugged her sister. "The good news is, we've got each other."

Eleanor handed her father his coffee and sat next to him, and said that she and Robin and Ravi would like to have a little talk with him.

"My hip's fine," Big Louis said. "Just fine."

Eleanor said, "That's wonderful, Dad. But this isn't about your hip—"

Big Louis interrupted her. "This about the goddamn easements?"

"That's no longer an issue," Eleanor said. "We've all eased our properties, as we agreed."

Big Louis seemed surprised. "All of you?"

"Yup, all," Robin said. "Three of a kind. I signed the papers yesterday. And I've changed my mind about selling the house, too. I think I'm needed here in Levi Lamb to help Eleanor look after you and help Ravi raise his adorable kids. Being Aunt Robin has become important to me in so many new ways. End of report."

"And, we're not here to talk about our deer fence either," Ravi said. "That case is closed, too. We're not going to build it. Instead, I'll give Jeter a pill once a month to keep him tick-free and watch the kids like a hawk. Realistically, that's the best I can do."

"So, Dad, as you can see, we've been trying to get your kingdom in order, to tie up as many loose ends as we can," Eleanor said. "Now, we'd like to talk with you about your accident—"

"I just told you, my hip's fine. My nurse says so, too."

Eleanor hesitated as she mustered the courage to tell her father that he couldn't live with her forever. She began by saying that she was delighted that his hip was healing so quickly but added, in as loving a fashion as she could, that eventually he'd have to move.

When he asked if Eleanor was throwing him out, Robin answered for her. "Far from it, Dad. What Eleanor is trying to tell you is that you'd be better off living somewhere where you can get help immediately if something like this happens again."

Big Louis gave Robin a dark look. "Never. No way. I'll go back to my house, and I'll be fine, thank you, just fine."

"Dad, we're only trying to do what makes the most sense for you," Robin said.

"How can I trust you to be sensible? Of all people; with all your—"

"Whoa, Mr. McCutchen," Ravi said. "Let's stay on point here and approach this situation like businessmen, the way you would have solved a problem like this when you were a leader at Gillette."

Big Louis nodded and turned to look at his son-in-law.

"Good. So, let's start with the facts." Ravi smiled. "Remember the businessman's code? In God we trust, all others must bring facts and data?"

Big Louis nodded again. "I like that."

Ravi continued. "Me, too, and the facts are that since your wife died, you haven't had a partner to keep you company, to look after you."

"You're goddamn well right," Big Louis said. "And I still miss her."

"I understand, sir," Ravi said. "Please remember, I just lost my wife, too, so I know what you're feeling."

Big Louis' hands trembled as he wiped tears from his cheeks, and he said that he was sorry.

"Moreover, you're a month away from your seventy-ninth birthday, and you've just had two scary incidents that required other people to help you, and there's no guarantee that, at your age, you won't have others." Ravi smiled at Big Louis. "Knowing you, sir, I think you'd agree that you're no spring chicken."

Big Louis sat a little straighter. "No spring chicken?" He laughed. "I like that."

"Also, your house was designed for you and your daughters a long while back, not for a single person your age," Ravi said. "You know, with the bedroom on the second floor, things like that. So, here's what Robin and Eleanor and I are proposing, and I've gotten The Cliffs to agree to it all."

"Never. That goddamned place? Never."

"Please, Mr. McCutchen, hear me out. It's all good. We've reserved a two-bedroom cottage for you that we think will make you very happy. It's all on one floor and has a patio with a view of the great range. What's more, you can have Tray live with you, and there's plenty of room for you to run him. And you'll come out ahead of the game financially. Robin thinks you should get $750,000, or even more—"

Big Louis interrupted. "What about the puppy?"

"We thought taking care of two of them might be too much, so, if it's okay with you, I'd love to take Blanche," Robin said. "I could use the company with the boys away at school and with Henry . . ." She paused. "Plus, I can bring her to visit you and Tray anytime you'd like."

Big Louis frowned and looked at Robin, then Ravi, and last at Eleanor. "Really? I can keep Tray and look at the mountains? For sure?"

"For sure," Ravi answered.

"Absolutely," Eleanor said.

"Guaranteed, Dad," Robin said, "or your money back."

Big Louis continued to look from one to another as though they'd just joined the discussion. Finally, he asked, "We all done?"

Ravi chuckled. "Not quite yet, sir. We'd like to hear what you think, how you feel about all of this. And if you have any questions."

Big Louis stared at the floor. "When would this happen?"

"As soon as you've finished your physical therapy," Eleanor said.

"And you won't have a thing to worry about," Robin said. "The Cliffs will move you out and in, and I'll handle selling your house."

"Okay, but I'd like to spend one more night in my camp. To say goodbye.'

"Sounds like a plan," Ravi said. "It's a new beginning for you and all of us."

"And know this too, Dad," Eleanor said, "we'll always be here for you."

Big Louis shrugged. "A new beginning? Well, I'll be god-damned. That include the Red Sox?"

"If that's what it takes," Ravi said, "I'll get on it right away."

After Robin and Ravi left, Eleanor called from the kitchen, "You comfortable, Dad? Want to take a nap? Or more coffee?"

Big Louis said he'd like another cup with cream, no sugar.

Eleanor placed his coffee on the table next to him and joined him on the couch. "Whew! Quite a morning, huh?"

"If you say so," her father said and began to wring his hands. Eleanor reached for his hands to quiet him.

When Big Louis seemed to calm, Eleanor started to let go but changed her mind. "I like holding hands with you. It makes me feel like a little girl again."

Her father nodded but didn't speak.

Eleanor gave his hands a gentle squeeze. "Dad, there is one other thing I'd like to talk with you about." Big Louis tried to pull his hands free and started to say something, but Eleanor interrupted him. "Relax, Dad. Please. This isn't about easements or The Cliffs or anything like that. It's about April and me. Remember, my friend April in Saranac Lake?"

Big Louis looked puzzled. "The one who makes me laugh?"

"Good for you," Eleanor said. "She's the one who makes me laugh, too, and once you're in your new home, she's going to move in with me."

"Doesn't surprise me. The road between here and Saranac's closed more than it's open in the winter."

Eleanor laughed. "You're funny, Dad. The road's not the only reason she's moving. We want to live together. You know, be partners?"

"Like a law firm?"

Eleanor didn't know if her father was really as out of it as he appeared or that, down deep, he'd known that she was gay all along. She wondered if he was having one of his occasional lucid moments and was baiting her to make the conversation as difficult for her as possible. But, she thought, there was no turning back now. "Uh, no, April's not a lawyer. She's a graphic designer. Our partnership is different than a law firm. It's based on love."

"And, trust, I hope."

"And trust."

"That's good," her father said, "because partnerships never work without trust."

Again, Eleanor wasn't sure that her father understood what she was telling him but thought she'd gone far enough, at least for the moment. "So, you approve, Dad?"

"Of course, I approve," Big Louis said. "You've always been my favorite."

TWENTY-NINE

Robin worried that she might not be able to sell her father's camp for the $750,000 that Ravi had promised and hurried home to fine-tune her analysis. She made herself a coffee, called Blanche to join her, and sat at her desk. The lighted panel on her answering machine indicated that she had two messages. The first caller had paused for a moment without speaking and hung up. Robin deleted the call, thinking that something odd was going on, that she'd had three similar hang-ups in the past two days. She listened for the second call, and her heart began to race when she heard Henry's voice: "Hi. I've been calling but wanted to talk with you rather than leave a message. But here goes. I'm working my way north and am coming home. I'm not really sure what I was running from. I didn't kill that Groves guy and will try to straighten that out when I get home. Mostly, though, I've learned a lot about myself. No, correct that. I've learned how much you and Little Louis and Hobey mean to me. How much I love you. All of you. But, please, please, don't tell anyone until I'm back and we've had time to chat. Not even your sisters or the boys. That's all I ask. That and that you'll take me back. Okay. There it is. See you soon."

Robin stared at the answering machine and began to cry. "Holy shit. Finally, my prayers have been answered. It's a deal, Honeybunch. I promise. Mum's the word." She wiped at her tears and hit the REPLAY button to hear Henry's voice again, to make sure she wasn't dreaming.

THIRTY

Robin and Eleanor watched the movers load a carton of books into their van, saying that they'd be back the next day to finish up. The house the McCutchen girls had once called home, where they sought refuge after their mother's death until they went away to college, was now empty. More than just empty, it was stripped of its personality. With no pictures on the walls, no hunting clothes or lanyards hanging from crude wood pegs, and no rugs or curtains, every sound was magnified, and the space looked cavernous, so much larger than either of them ever remembered.

When they'd finished dinner, the sisters helped Big Louis up the stairs to his bedroom, where Eleanor turned down the bed-clothes and said, "All set?"

"For what?" Big Louis asked.

"For your new life, your new home," Eleanor said.

"And, what, again, was wrong with my old one?"

Eleanor said there wasn't anything wrong with it, but he'd have far fewer things to worry about in his new life.

"Fewer worries for you or me?" he asked.

"For everybody," Robin said. "It's a family win-win."

Big Louis sat on the bed, clutching the small canvas duffle he'd packed for his last night in his camp, but didn't respond.

Eleanor frowned at Robin and asked if he was changing his mind.

Big Louis wrung his hands and asked if it would make any difference.

"Good question," Robin said. She laid a hand on his to quiet his nervous twisting and clasping. "Let's give it a try and see how it goes. Okay?"

Big Louis looked out the bedroom window into the inky darkness and muttered, "You know I'm a foolish old dog? Right?"

Neither sister had any idea where this question was coming from nor where it might lead. Robin tried to follow Big Louis' line of thought as diplomatically as she could. "An elderly dog with a brilliant pedigree, but not foolish."

"And Eleanor, you know one other thing?" he asked.

"Another thing?" Eleanor said.

"I owe you an apology for doubting you around your easement."

"Thanks, Dad, but it wasn't the easement situation that hurt me so badly," Eleanor said. "It was doubting that I loved you, doubting that what I wanted was best for you."

"Well, there's that, too," Big Louis said.

Eleanor asked if there was anything more.

"You're goddamn right there's more. Do you forgive me?"

Eleanor leaned toward him and kissed him on the cheek. "Of course, I forgive you."

"So, I've been a good father?"

"Is that question for both of us or just for Ellie?" Robin asked.

"I'm asking you both."

"Okay, then, this one's on me, Babycakes," Robin said. "You've been better than good; you've been great. But, let's face it, you're not perfect, but then again, no one is. The bakers took all of us out of the oven a little too early. The important thing is that you've tried hard to be the best you could be, and that's all anyone can ask."

"That's it?" Big Louis said.

Robin leaned forward to kiss him good night. "That's it."

Eleanor smoothed his hair and fluffed up his pillow before she kissed him. "As you always used to say, Dad, you'll be snug as a bug in a rug."

As they turned to leave, both said, "Love you."

Big Louis nodded and muttered, "I pray to God you mean it."

Once he was sure his daughters were well on their way home, Big Louis unzipped his duffle and took out a small yellow-lined pad and a pen. He left his Dopp kit, his pajamas, and his shiny Smith & Wesson snub-nosed revolver in the duffle and set it on his pillow.

THIRTY-ONE

A little before 8:00 the following morning, Eleanor went to Big Louis' camp to make his breakfast and help him finish packing before taking Tray and him to The Cliffs. Robin, Ravi, Owen, and Sgt. Oswald arrived within minutes of her call, closely followed by an ambulance from the Elizabethtown Community Hospital. To add to the confusion and hysteria, the movers soon pulled in to pick up Big Louis' bed and the odds and ends they'd left behind the day before.

Visibly shaken, the color having drained from her face, Eleanor blocked the front door and pleaded with her family and Owen not to go in the house. Without describing what she'd found, she repeatedly said, "Please don't go in there. Please. It's horrible, and it wouldn't do any good. It's an image that would be hard to erase."

Sgt. Oswald approached the group and asked that they do as Ms. McCutchen advised and clear the entrance so that he and the EMTs could assess what had happened.

Ravi wrapped Eleanor in a bear hug, as much to comfort her as to keep her from collapsing, and led her toward the dog kennels.

"Let it go," he said. "Let it go, Eleanor. Every little bit of it. It helps. I know. It helps."

Eleanor began pounding his chest with her fists. "First, Mom, then Julia, and now Dad. Does it never end?"

"Julia would scold me for asking, but did he leave a note?" Ravi said.

Eleanor dug a crumpled piece of yellow paper from a pocket in her blue jeans and handed it to him. She apologized, saying that Robin had balled it up in disgust when she'd read it.

Robin and Eleanor—

It seems I've lost almost everything, and I want to be with your mother so badly. My life is meaningless without her, and I'm the reason that she's no longer with us. Please tell the grandkids how much I love them. There's nothing left for me here. I belong with your mother.

I'm sorry.

When Ravi finished reading, he folded the paper neatly. "I think you should save this for the police, but there aren't any surprises here. It's efficient, business-like, and plagued with guilt. A pretty good snapshot of your dad."

Eleanor wiped tears from her cheeks and shook her head. "I don't know, Ravi. I just don't know. I'm so mad at him for not letting us help him and for what he's now done to us, but when I think how much he must have been suffering all these years, I feel so sorry for him. And I feel like I let him down."

"First off, you sure as hell didn't let him down," Ravi said. "And, for God's sake, please, no regrets. Your father's regrets are what killed him, and you don't want to get caught in that spiral."

While Ravi and Eleanor talked, Owen walked Robin the length of Big Louis' long dirt drive. "Jesus, Owen, his note, his fucking note," Robin said. "He said there wasn't anything left for him here. What are Eleanor and I? And you? And his grandkids? Chopped liver?"

"Don't take it too literally," Owen said. "He was confused. A lot of times, his thoughts were jumbled. I know he adored all three of you. Don't think for a moment that he didn't. He had such a hard time expressing his true feelings; it's a wonder your mom ever married him."

"But, doing this when he was about to start a new chapter of his life that might make him happy? What's with that? And, rather than going along with us, why couldn't he level with us and just say 'no'?" Robin paused. "Oh, sweet Jesus, Owen, you don't think he secretly planned it all along?"

"Maybe, but it doesn't make any difference. What's done is done, and life goes on. You're lucky that you've got each other to lean on."

Robin wrapped her arms around his neck and pressed her cheek against his. "You're the best friend a girl ever had, a family ever had, for that matter. We're all going to need you to lean on, too, so don't quit on us now."

"Don't give it a second thought," Owen said. "I'm not going anywhere."

As the EMTs wheeled Big Louis, strapped and wrapped in a shiny black bodybag, into their emergency vehicle, Robin began to cry again. "Well, Babycakes, here we are, two middle-aged orphans. God, but I'll miss him."

"Won't we all?" Eleanor said and embraced her. "The good news is we've got each other."

"You are so right," Robin said. "*Unus pro omnibus, omnes pro uno*."

Sgt. Oswald assured them that there was little left for them to do and suggested that they take a break from the depressing scene. As he said goodbye, he turned to Robin. "Give my regards to your husband. He must be happy now that the trout season's open."

At first, Robin thought he was kidding but quickly realized that this squared-away officer of the law wasn't one to kid, especially in circumstances like this; that in his awkward fashion, he was trying to ease their sadness with a personal gesture. "Don't you know?" Robin said. "Henry disappeared right after you ran the DNA test on him, and I haven't heard from him since."

The trooper flinched. "You've got to be kidding, Mrs. Honeywell. I had no idea. Why in the world did he do that?"

"He thought you suspected him of killing Jordan Groves."

"Really? The case was closed in December. Right after Thanksgiving, a couple who'd been picnicking near Nye Brook came forward to say that they'd seen a man who met Groves' description bushwhacking in the direction of Adrian's Abyss all by himself. Groves' death was listed as accidental."

"Perfect," Robin said. "Dead solid, fucking perfect."

"Ma'am?" the sergeant said.

"Nothing," Robin said. "I'm sure Henry will be glad to hear that if we ever see him again."

"I'm sure he will," Sgt. Oswald said as he set his flat-brimmed Stetson on the passenger seat of his cruiser and offered his condolences again.

EPILOGUE

On his drive back to his barracks, Sgt. Oswald wondered how the communication lines had failed so miserably, both for him and the Honeywell family. *What could he do to right the wrong?* He knew how much the news of Louis Mc-Cutchen's death would unsettle the Adirondack community and was surprised to feel a personal connection to the Honeywells. Maybe it was Robin's amusing burning of the hamburgers or Henry's innocent lies to protect his wife; it didn't matter. All he knew as he approached Ray Brook was that he was truly sorry for their loss.

As Owen climbed into his truck, he told the sisters that he'd check in with them in a few hours, that he needed to be with his wife for a while, to decompress around the loss of a man who for twenty years had been his idol and closest friend. He assured them that he'd visit the Hodgepodge on the way home to bring the staff up to date and make sure that all was in order. As Robin and Eleanor would say, "Owen being Owen."

Ravi left his father-in-law's camp to tell Kasun, Hansi, and Sara that their grandfather had died, thinking that this was the second time in a few months that his children had heard devastating news from him, and he prayed that he could help them with all their fears and questions. Suddenly he was overwhelmed by the need to have Julia at his side once again, and tears blurred his vision as he headed home.

Eleanor said she thought Tray would be as confused as the rest of the family by what had just happened and took the now masterless Llewellin with her. She drove slowly to her studio, eager to be by herself and talk with April, to tell her that, just in time, she'd been honest with her father about their relationship, and to let her know once again how glad she was that she would be moving in with her, that she needed her in the most desperate way.

Robin returned to her empty house, where she tried to collect her thoughts. She made a coffee, collapsed on the couch, and encouraged Blanche to sit next to her. She stroked the young Llewellin, saying she needed someone to talk to. "I've lost so damn many family members I love. It's been just horrible. First, my mom." She lifted Blanche's chin to look her in the eyes.

"Then my Honeybunch, who ran away for no reason at all. Then my gentle Julia. And today, your master and mine, my dad. So what do I tell Little Louis and Hobey? *How* do I tell them? It's a nightmare, Blanche. A fucking nightmare."

She stood and picked up the phone and stared blankly out the window. She drew a deep breath before dialing her sons at Groton when something caught her eye. She hung up the phone, wondering who the hell was wandering on her property today, of all days? She opened the front door and stepped outside to get a better look.

A familiar figure stood at the foot of the drive with a backpack slung over his shoulder and a yellow dog at his side. When the man saw her, he spread his arms as though he was signaling that he'd caught a large fish or as though he was inviting Robin to welcome him home.

The Witness

The war in Bosnia began on April 6, 1992, when Bosnia-Herzegovina proclaimed its independence from the Yugoslav Federation. That same day, Serbian paramilitary units and the Yugoslav People's Army attacked Sarajevo with the threat of a war that would "lead Bosnia-Herzegovina into hell and perhaps make the Muslim people disappear." Thus began a brutal struggle for sovereignty, territory, and ethnic autonomy /superiority that eventually included Bosnian Croat forces, a conflict known for its indiscriminate shelling of cities and towns, ethnic cleansing, torture, and mass rapes. Peace was finally declared in December 1995, but not until over 100,000 people had been killed and close to two million displaced from their homes.

The horror that the Siege of Sarajevo would eventually shower upon its citizens was made indelibly clear by the killing of twenty-two civilians and the wounding of one hundred and eight more innocents as they stood in line waiting to buy bread shortly after the war began. This is where Jusuf Kurtovic's story begins.

J USUF KURTOVIC HAS NO IDEA why he's driven to buy bread on a balmy May morning in 1992. Perhaps it's an act of defiance. He'll be damned if he will let the bearded bastards in the hills who took his son from him in the early days of the war further disrupt his life. Perhaps it's because he fears for the safety of his daughter-in-law and his granddaughters, thinking that at sixty-eight, he's led a full life and if anything goes wrong while shopping, it would be better if it happens to him than them. Or, perhaps it's for no reason other than every Wednesday for as long as he can remember he's enjoyed visiting the bakery on the Vase Miskina pedestrian mall.

Whatever the reason, Jusuf chooses a route to the bakery that minimizes the chance of being the target of a sniper's bullet. A few minutes before 10:00, a long line has formed well ahead of him. He thinks so many will risk so much for the promise of fresh bread when a loud whistling sound warns of approaching mortar shells. Three deafening explosions follow, wreaking havoc, dismemberment, and death.

Oblivious to the additional rounds that could target him, Jusuf rushes to the carnage. Amidst the moaning, the wails of horror and disbelief, survivors running and turning in circles, not sure who needs help the most or what to do, he stumbles over bodies and body parts and slips on pools of blood. Once the Red Cross volunteers arrive, he helps carry litters, holds IVs, and eases the walking-wounded into the cars that wait to take them to the Kosevo Hospital.

When he returns home, his face, hands, and clothes smeared with blood, his daughter-in-law takes one look at him and bursts into tears. "Thank God, you're alive. All I could think of was first Emir and now you." She wipes at her tears and asks if he's been injured.

"I'm okay, but it was horrible, Leila, absolutely horrific. Worse than anything I saw during the war. At least twenty were killed, and God only knows how many more were injured. Those of us helping were told that the doctors at the trauma center are overwhelmed, that they've run out of anesthesia and blood." He collapses in a chair by the kitchen table. "What were those Chetnik bastards punishing us for? Our only crime was waiting in line for bread."

"It's so random, so unpredictable, but you're home, and you're okay," Leila says and sighs. "It's all too much for the girls and me." She pauses and nods as though she's answering a silent question. "But, Irma and Ema are okay. And I'm okay, Jusuf, I really am." She forces a smile. "Now, you should get cleaned up. But first, how about a little nip to take the edge off?"

"Brandy at lunchtime?" Jusuf says. "Why the hell not? But one thing is certain; I've lived a good life, Leila, longer than I deserve, and, starting tomorrow, I'll be getting all our food and water. It's not safe for you or the girls anymore. It's up to me. It's the least this old man can do."

∞

ALTHOUGH HIS MODEST STUCCO HOUSE is a kilometer from Sarajevo's center, Jusuf feels the ground shake as endless mortar rounds explode. In the four months since the siege has begun, he hasn't experienced anything like this, not even the shelling of the bakery. He calls to Leila and his granddaughters that he's going to see what's going on. The choking smell of smoke lingers in the humid August evening as he hurries to a high point in the street to look over the once serene city, now illuminated by flames engulfing the National Library.

Jusuf thinks that destroying the National Library is as predictable as the dawn, that the message is as clear and cruel as everything else the Serbs have set out to do. He watches the building where Bosnia stored and preserved its culture, the home to volumes of books reflecting life under the Ottoman and Austro-Hungarian empires and Yugoslavia before being reduced to rubble and ashes. He shakes his head in disgust. Of course, they'd target the Vijecnica. What could be a greater insult? But he still can't understand what motivates them. He is a Sarajevan, a Bosnian patriot, proud of his country's culture and its past. A few short months ago, his Serbian and Croatian friends felt the same. Or at least he thought they had. What baffles him most is those who have gone over to the other side so quickly and casually, as though they were changing a sweater. Their cruelty is boundless, beyond comprehension.

Someone slips an arm around his and takes his hand. Leila's touch is familiar and, as always, reassuring. He looks into her dark eyes that brim with tears.

"Vijecnica?" she asks.

"Vijecnica."

"Shameless."

Jusuf nods. "The symbol of our culture.'

"But, right now, please come home. Inhaling all that smoke can't be good for you."

"My lungs are fine. Just fine. And, before you ask, so's my heart."

Jusuf's dismissive tone when talking about his health or aging is all too familiar to Leila. She slips her arm around him and kisses him on the cheek. "Like father, like son. Both stubborn as mules."

Jusuf smiles. "And, with my medication, healthy as a horse."

As they turn to leave, he turns to his neighbor, who stands at his side. "It's hard to believe, Milan. Hard to comprehend."

Milan shrugs. "Maybe for you, Professor, but times have changed. For people like you, Sarajevo is now a dangerous place, and your son wasn't making you or your family any safer."

Jusuf flinches. "How does what Emir was doing differ from what many of us did during the war? How could fighting to save our country possibly be wrong?"

Milan pats him on the shoulder. "I'm not old enough to remember the war, but Bosnia's not your country anymore. So, be careful and get your family out of Sarajevo while you can." He looks to Leila. "Please, convince him that it's what's best for you and your daughters."

Jusuf shakes his head in disapproval, and an awkward silence follows. Both men return their gaze to the fire. Finally, Jusuf wraps an arm around Leila's shoulders and pulls her tight to him. "Let's go home. I've seen and heard enough here." He turns to his neighbor. "Good night, Milan. You take good care, too."

"Goodnight to you," Milan says. "And if you and your family want to be safe, Jusuf, I suggest you take my advice."

Jusuf takes one last look at the flames that belch skyward in bright orange waves. He thinks Sarajevans will remember this as the fire to end all fires. He stares at the simmering, smoking ruins of Vijecnica, then out across the Miljacka river and beyond to the hills where those who intend to destroy all he knows and loves are plotting their next attack. He cups his hands over his nose and mouth in horror as he watches the ashes of millions of books floating down upon Sarajevo like new falling snow.

Once home, a small wire-haired dog places its forepaws on Jusuf's thighs, wagging its short-cropped tail. As he stoops to scratch the dog's ears, he calls to his granddaughters. "It's okay, ladies, we're home."

The teenagers emerge from the basement clad in tee-shirts and blue jeans, ripped at the knees. "What's going on?" Irma asks.

Jusuf slumps on the piano bench and absent-mindedly lifts and lowers the fallboard that covers the piano's keys. "They're shelling Vijecnica. Nothing is sacred." He is having trouble hiding his anger, despair, and yes, his fear, not for himself, but for these promising and innocent girls and their mother. "I'm afraid they won't stop until they've destroyed everything and all of us. Not only useless old men like me but your mother and the two of you." He looks down at the small dog that lays at his feet. "And maybe Dzukela, too."

"They're not that sick," Ema says. "Please tell me they're not."

"If only I could," Jusuf says.

"Your Dedo is right," their mother says. "Life here is getting more and more dangerous by the day, and we no longer know who our friends are."

"Then why don't we leave?" Irma asks. "Go somewhere safe."

"Why do you always want to go to faraway places?" Ema says. "Besides, where would we go?"

Their mother surprises them by saying, "Maybe Zagreb with your cousins."

"No, Mom. Please, no," Ema says. "We'll be fine here. We'll be with our friends and our Dedo and Dzukela. We'll be careful. I promise."

"It's not just you," Leila says. "It's me, too. It would be so much easier if your father were here with us. I can't handle all of this by myself."

Jusuf reaches for Leila's hand. "You're doing fine. You're an incredible mother and a great comfort to me. We have a lot more thinking and talking to do, so let's get some sleep and try not to worry. Nothing can be decided tonight." He stands, kisses each girl and their mother goodnight, and tells them that he loves them all. On his way to his mattress in the cellar, he says that as dark as things seem at the moment, somehow things will get brighter. Things will work out.

THE FOLLOWING MORNING, Jusuf finishes eating a small portion of powdered eggs and a slice of bread and tells his granddaughters to eat up, that breakfast is the most important meal of the day.

Irma giggles. "That's what you said yesterday, Dedo."

"And the day before and the day before that," Ema says.

Jusuf says he assumes it must still be true because he hasn't heard anything to the contrary. His granddaughters look at him to see if he is teasing them. As a smile spreads across his face, they smile too.

Leila says she's sorry there isn't any coffee, that they're almost out of water, and suggests Jusuf go another day without shaving.

He shrugs and runs a hand over his white stubble. "Maybe I should let it grow like a guerilla, like a Chetnik. Sort of like a disguise."

"We'll love you no matter how you look," Leila says and turns on the radio. "Let's see what we can learn about the fire."

The news from Radio Sarajevo 202, the independent voice of the people, is delivered in a halting, dispassionate tone.

> The fire in the National and University Library—a symbol of what Sarajevo used to be and what many want it to be in the future—has raged all night and is still burning. The majestic structure that originally was our city hall is now no more than a smoldering shell, its insides completely destroyed by incendiary bombs. The lovely domed glass ceiling has shattered and collapsed onto the main floor.

The announcer's voice falters, but she continues.

> An estimated eighty percent of the library's collections, as many as three million books, including Aristotle, Hegel, and Kant's original writings, have been reduced to ash. Firefighters fought the flames as best they could, but their task was impossible. Snipers shot at them, and shells were lobbed at them by members of an army who, ironically, were once charged with protecting our city and its treasures. In the end, the firefighters were ordered to withdraw and let the fire burn itself out.

Jusuf switches the radio off to save its battery and shakes his head in disgust.

"Should we seriously consider Zagreb?" Leila asks.

The girls stare at their grandfather. They know that their mother will agree to whatever course he chooses. "Let's give it a little more time," Jusuf says. "I can't believe the UN, or the US for that matter will tolerate this much longer."

≫

LATER THAT AFTERNOON, Jusuf sets out for the brewery to collect water. He has slung a bag over his shoulder that holds two small plastic bottles and carries a four-liter bottle in each hand. As always, he's brought Dzukela with him to give him his only chance to go for a walk. The little dog trots close to him, shying away from the packs of starving strays that roam the streets, tearing at the garbage piles that litter every block. Everywhere Jusuf turns, there are signs that read "watch out, sniper." Thuds of exploding mortar rounds replace the music of the bird songs that once were common on the now almost treeless streets. Scores of abandoned cars are riddled by machine-gun fire, their windshields cracked or missing. The façades of most buildings, even historic landmarks like Vijecnica, are pockmarked with bullet holes, their black-eyed windows covered with plastic. Many have collapsed into piles of rocky rubble. In contrast, others are roofless, with cables and wires stretching across empty open spaces like tightropes.

White Toyota 4-Runners with large black **UN** stenciled on their doors seem to pass at every intersection. His once vibrant Sarajevo is now a ghost town.

And Sarajevo roulette—the ultimate guessing game—begins once again. Jusuf stops on the sidewalk of Zmaja od Bosne, the Dragon of Bosnia Street, nicknamed "Sniper Alley" by foreign journalists. Although smoke from the burning library has drawn a filmy curtain between Jusuf and the sun, the temperature has risen to an unseasonably warm 77°. As he wipes sweat from his brow, the distant pop-pop-pop of machine-gun fire seems to punctuate the pre-recorded call to prayer.

He turns and looks at a young man—nothing more than a boy really—who paces away from him and then back, trying to will himself to cross the intersection. The boy adjusts the crude rope harness that holds his water bottles and, for an instant, returns

Jusuf's glance. "You think they'll pause during prayers? I mean, do you think it's safe to go now?"

The boy reminds Jusuf of his son Emir at his age, strong and confident yet respectful, and he wants to assure him that he knows when it's safe and when it isn't. Except he doesn't. All he knows is that it's never safe, that there is no rhyme or reason when they decide to shoot or at whom. Unarmed men, women, children; all are fair game. Finally, Jusuf says, "Now would be as good a time as any. But run like hell."

The boy draws a deep breath and sprints across the intersection. He runs like an athlete, smoothly and effortlessly and with great speed. Jusuf braces himself for the shot that will end this display of youthful promise. No shot is fired, and the boy hurdles the far curb out of harm's way. He puts his hands on his knees to catch his breath, calls a blessing to Jusuf, and trots away.

"My turn," Jusuf says. He looks to see if anyone can hear him talking to himself but doesn't give a damn if there is. It's his right at his age. He figures it will take him at least three times longer than it did the boy and debates when to go when a woman approaches him. He straightens his posture as she reaches his side, privately laughing at himself, wondering what a woman could want with an old man like him.

"Good afternoon, Professor," the woman says. Before he can return her greeting, she adds, "No, you don't know me, if that's what you're going to ask. I've seen you play many times with the symphony." She smiles up at him and then stares at the deserted intersection, her bright green eyes full of life. "I'm going to the market to see if I can find some bread. There hasn't been any for over a week. And you?"

Jusuf thinks she exudes self-confidence, that she's delicate and alarmingly attractive. Although silver streaks highlight her closely cropped black hair, she can't be much older than Leila; maybe fifty at the most. "I'm getting water, and whatever there is at the bakery if anything."

She continues to stare at the street. "Be careful. Vase Miskin is very dangerous."

"I know, only too well," Jusuf says. "I was nearby when the shelling started."

"Lucky, lucky you," the woman says. "At least those not so lucky had that brave cellist to honor them."

Jusuf smiles. "Vedran Smailovic, playing Albinoni's Adagio in G minor, a day for every person killed and in his tuxedo, no less. Typical Vedran. I miss him a lot."

"Why, of course, you know all about him," the woman says. "How stupid of me."

"Yes," Jusuf says. "I mean, yes, I know him well, but, no, you're not stupid."

The woman laughs. "You're a diplomat and a kind man, Professor Kurtovic."

Jusuf thanks her but thinks that right now he has more important things on his mind than his old friend Vedran, like how to get across the intersection safely. He hesitates. "I'm going. If they shoot at me, I doubt they'll waste a bullet on you."

He gives Dzukela's leash a gentle tug and begins to run. Halfway across the intersection, he hears the snap of a bullet and then the rifle's report. He tries to run faster and wonders why the Chetniks waste ammunition on older people like him who aren't a threat to them. The sniper appears to save his next bullet for a more deserving person and doesn't try to kill him again.

The woman waiting to cross calls to him. "You're leading a charmed life, Professor. In case you care, my name is Sandra Fazlic. I come this way every four days. Maybe we'll meet again.

Until then, I wish you well. And, by the way, you run like a duck."

His clumsy running is the result of his right leg being mangled by shrapnel during WW II, and he laughs at her comment but mainly as a release from the fact that he's just narrowly escaped being killed. He kneels to let his heart slow and to comfort Dzukela, saying to his little companion, "She certainly is forward. Has a Sarajevo sense of humor. Who knows, one day she might become a friend."

He thinks the Seher-Cehaja is the safest bridge to cross the Miljacka and trudges up the hill to the spring at Sarajevsko pivara, the old brewing company. Even though it's only a short distance from the sniper pit on Mount Trebevic, its basement proves to be impenetrable to the persistent shelling, and its springs continue to provide water through the many hoses that now run to the street.

He stands in the shortest line and waits patiently, consumed by how close he's just come to becoming a meaningless statistic. When his turn comes, he sets his bottles on the ground and reaches for the spigot when a large hand clamps his, and a burly man dressed in a dark camouflage uniform says, "No. No, Professor. Let me, please. You shouldn't risk those talented hands on work like this."

Jusuf is both surprised and delighted. This is the second time someone has recognized him for his role with the Philharmonic, and it comforts him no end. He thinks the war has stolen so many people's identity and dignity and worries that he and the orchestra are no more than a dim memory since the siege has stopped them from performing. "Thank you. You're very kind," he says. "Figuring out how much water to carry is becoming more of an art than a science. I'm afraid I'm getting weaker and soon won't be able to carry four full bottles home."

The soldier suggests that he bring a friend to help him.

"Good idea, except most of my friends have fled to Berlin or Vienna. Or worse, if you know what I mean."

"I know what you mean, sir," the soldier says. "Your son was a good man and friend of mine."

Jusuf reaches to shake the man's hand and asks his name.

"Vidic. Aron Vidic."

"Well, thank you, Aron Vidic," Jusuf says. "Your comment about Emir means the world to me."

AT HOME, Jusuf turns on his small transistor radio and moves it around the kitchen table to improve reception. He says to Leila, "I find something comforting in . . . in what's her name's friendly voice, especially when she's reporting on events other than the killing."

"Her name is Lana Ulak, and I especially like her humorous comments."

"Me, too. She reminds me of your mother-in-law and her endless, funny stories."

Leila smiles. "She always said it was the Irish in her."

Jusuf kisses his daughter-in-law on the cheek. "And she always said that we were blessed to have you in our family. Now, let's see what our girlfriend has to say today."

The reporter begins with local coverage.

A water tap has been opened on a small street off of Radomir Putnik Boulevard, and a line is forming before the tap is shut off again. If you're interested, now's the time to go. And now's also the time for today's big story, the results of last year's census. The population of

Bosnia-Herzegovina is now almost 4.4 million, with 527,000 living here in Sarajevo. Ninety-two percent of B-H is comprised of three nationalities: Muslims, about 44%; Serbs, 31%; and Croats, 17%. Each may have strikingly different political aspirations, but all three have one thing in common; we all speak dialects of the same Slavic language, Serbo-Croatian."

Jusuf flashes back to the census questionnaire. Although he considers himself a religious skeptic who admits to attending midnight mass on Christmas because it's a popular thing to do, he chose "Muslim" to avoid identifying as Serbian or Croat. His thoughts are interrupted by the announcer's shift in topic.

Now some international news. Based on articles in the London tabloids, the Prince and Princess of Wales are rumored to be separating.

And, finally, here's something to lighten your day. A woman was visited by a friend. The woman asked if her friend would like a cup of coffee. When the guest answered, "No thanks," the woman said, "Good. Now I can take a shower."

"Funny, but so true," Leila says as the broadcaster signs off in her familiar fashion:

On this 150th day of the siege, September 20th, 1992, 583 Sarajevan civilians have been killed or reported missing, and nearly a million Bosnians have been displaced from their homes. Until tomorrow, this is Lana Ulak for Radio Sarajevo 202, urging you to be careful and safe and find a little joy in your life.

Jusuf turns off the radio. "No one wants to speculate on how long this damn war will last."

"Because no one really knows," Leila says. "What harm would it do to get the girls out of here, even if it's only for a short time until it's safe once again?"

"Zagreb?"

"Why not? They get along well with their cousins, and their schooling there would be more dependable. Plus, there'd be more food."

Jusuf knows that even though the UN guarantees safe passage on their "Blue Corridors," getting out of Sarajevo requires connections with a humanitarian organization and some pretty hefty bribes. "I'll write Ivan and Sara to see what they advise. The thought of you leaving makes me miss the three of you already, but what's best for you comes first."

IN LESS THAN A MONTH, Jusuf says that, surprisingly, he's heard back from the Novaks. The girls and their mother stop eating their sparse dinners and quietly place their forks on their plates. The letter, Jusuf says, is typical of Ivan; very loving but firm. "He said that the idea of you living with them makes Sara and him worry about their safety. It makes him 'Nervous as hell,' as he put it. The tension with you being Muslims would be palpable, and all of you, but mainly you girls, would feel it. You simply couldn't avoid it. He said a sign outside the school reads 'No Dogs or Muslims Allowed.' If that isn't enough, he knows from experience that you'd be teased about being refugees." He pauses and takes a breath. "What's more, because the Croatian government doesn't want any more foreigners in their schools, Ivan says there's a good chance you'd be refused entry into the country. He ended his comments, writing that while the fighting hasn't spread to Zagreb, it's all that anyone can think or talk about."

"So we're not going to Zagreb?" Ema asks.

Jusuf nods. "It may even be impossible, but it'll be dangerous for sure."

"Shouldn't we at least try?" Irma asks.

"Please, Irma, your Uncle Ivan is a very thoughtful and caring man, and he strongly advises against us going," Leila says. "I think we must accept it and get on the best we can here, as a family."

Irma looks to her grandfather. "If you're sure, I know we shouldn't go."

Jusuf smiles at her. "I'm sure, and heaven only knows if you'd ever be allowed back home." He smiles. "Hopefully, things will get better here soon, and I'll have my family around me."

"And if they don't get better?" Leila asks.

Jusuf sighs. "There are other options, not particularly good ones, but let's give it some more time."

AT THE INTERSECTION where Jusuf first met her, Sandra stands against a shipping container that has been put in place to provide protection from snipers. She is more beautiful than he remembers, and he laughs when she says, "We've got to stop meeting like this, Professor."

He feels like a schoolboy, unable to think how to respond, and asks how she is faring.

"Fighting the good fight, but aren't we all?" She reminds him that her name is Sandra Fazlic.

"Jusuf."

Sandra smiles. "Well, now that we've got that awkward part out of the way, where are you headed today, Jusuf?"

"The brewery."

She asks if she can tag along.

Jusuf says he'd like that and will make a run for it whenever she's ready.

"I'm as ready as I'll ever be. Say a prayer."

Jusuf reaches for her hand, clucks at Dzukela, and, on the count of three, all race across the intersection. Not a single shot is fired.

"Perhaps they've lost interest in us," Sandra says. "Perhaps they have bigger fish to fry."

"Who knows?" Jusuf says. "This morning, they killed a little boy and girl on an orphanage bus on its way out of the city. It should be pretty clear by now; they'd like to kill us all unless we die from hunger or the cold first."

"Please don't talk that way," Sandra says. "It upsets me."

As they approach the Seher-Cehaja, Jusuf stops abruptly and turns Sandra to him. The bloated corpses of a man and woman lay head-to-toe on the sidewalk at the foot of the bridge. "Don't look," he says. "For God's sake, don't look."

Sandra squeezes his arm. "I had to claim my husband's body after the fighting at the Canton Building. Nothing could be worse than that."

For a moment, Jusuf looks away from her. "I lost my son in the early days as well."

"So, you understand?"

"I understand." He thinks that the loss continues indefinitely, that the story has no end. He is surprised to feel tears beginning to well. Has he found someone who knows what it was like for him for his son to disappear? Without being able to say good-bye? Without being able to give him a proper burial?

"You and I are victims of this idiotic war, as well," Sandra says. She runs a comb through her short-cropped hair and puts on lipstick. "All set. Let's go."

Jusuf gives her a questioning look. "Isn't it an odd time to do that?"

"Not really. It's what many of us do. We try to look well turned out for the Chetniks, whether in a face-to-face confrontation or through the scopes on their rifles. It's our way of telling them that they haven't conquered us." She smiles. "Besides, if a sniper gets me, I want to die looking my very best."

They cross the bridge and hurry up the hill to the brewery. Unlike most days, only a handful of people wait for their turn at the spigots. The burly guard who had been Emir's friend waves and signals to Jusuf to join him.

"Have they been there long, Aron?" Jusuf asks.

"The bodies?" Aron shrugs. "It's been two days. No one will accept responsibility for them. Not even the UN."

"Makes you wonder who's doing what to whom," Sandra says.

"No need to wonder," Aron says. "Nothing is beyond these people. They kill their friends and family members if they don't support their cause."

ONCE THEY'VE COLLECTED all the water they can carry and have made their way to the city's old bazaar, Jusuf asks if he can help Sandra take her bottles home. "Always the gentleman," she says. "But I'll be fine. Perhaps some other time?"

Jusuf wants to say that he'd like that, that he'd like it very much. Instead, he says, "Yes. Perhaps some other time."

WHEN HIS GRANDDAUGHTERS FINISH another breakfast of powdered eggs and a slice of bread—still "the most important meal of the day," according to Jusuf—he sits at the piano.

In turn, Ema adopts a serious posture and asks Irma, "Can you tell me how to get to Carnegie Hall?"

"Of course. Practice, practice, practice," Irma says, and both girls and their mother laugh at one of Jusuf's often-repeated jokes.

Jusuf smiles and rubs his hands to warm them. As he begins to play, Irma says, "Oh, good, Shostakovich."

He nods. "To cheer you."

"Concerto number two, right, Dedo?" Ema asks.

Jusuf nods again.

The girls sit quietly at the kitchen table. Jusuf's music has become their music, as much a part of their lives as the shelling and the sniper fire. He finishes to applause and thanks them, telling them that, as always, they're his best audience.

At ten o'clock, he switches on the radio for the day's news.

In case you need reminding, today, November 25th, is Statehood Day, the day in 1943 that we, as a people, agreed that our country was home to Serbs, Croats, and Bosnians. Yes, Bosnians too. And, now, look what's happened. Over the past 24 hours, 43 civilians have been killed and 79 wounded. The victims weren't fighting anybody; their only wrongdoing was living in Sarajevo. The world wouldn't tolerate events like this in Paris, London, or New York, so on Statehood Day, I have to ask: why is Sarajevo any different?

"Statehood Day?" Jusuf switches off the radio and turns to Leila. "What in the world has our country come to?"

"It's difficult to understand," Leila says. "It's even more confusing for the girls. In many ways, they're being robbed of their teenage years, years they'll never be able to recapture." She shrugs. "It is what it is. That gloomy picture aside, we've got to eat. It's time to try to do a little stocking up. The stuff from the humanitarian relief was better than nothing. But three cans of tuna fish, two kilos of pasta, three kilos of potatoes, and a gallon of milk won't feed us for six weeks."

"It's no wonder 40,000 Sarajevans are malnourished," Jusuf says. He pulls on his parka and hooks a leash to Dzukela's collar. "I'm off to the market to see what I can find."

DZUKELA LEAPS THROUGH THE SNOW on the unplowed streets as Jusuf trudges toward the once-thriving Pijaca Markale. A block from the market, a woman calls his name. "Is that you, Professor? With the beard, you look like Papa Hemingway."

"At least you didn't mistake me for a Chetnik," Jusuf says.

"On the contrary," Sandra says. "You're very handsome."

She flushes when he says she looks lovely in her long mink coat. "I'm embarrassed to say, but it's the warmest coat I own. Are you headed to the Markale?"

Jusuf says he is.

She offers him her arm. "Would you like some company?"

"Live for the moment, as if you only have a few moments left. Right?"

"Wrong, Jusuf, that's too fatalistic. Optimism is our most precious asset for survival, so please don't talk like that."

Jusuf looks at his boots and kicks at the snow. "Of course, you're right, but there are times . . ."

He pulls her arm tight against his side and walks without speaking to the market entrance, where Sandra says, "Be prepared. The black market prices are higher than ever. A pound of coffee is twenty-five times what it used to be."

They wander arm in arm, stopping at each stand, debating what they need rather than what they want. Jusuf buys three small tins of German frankfurters, the only remaining loaf of bread, powdered milk, and a half dozen candles.

Sandra also buys a handful of candles, plus a can of tuna fish and a pound of coffee. When she offers to buy Jusuf two Bear Paw pastries, he says, "For twenty Deutschmarks each?"

She smiles up at him. "As a special treat. To cheer you up."

"That's way too much money."

"I agree, but one thing I have is lots of money; money but no influence. All that disappeared with the death of my husband. Besides, what is it they always say, you can't take it with you?"

Jusuf laughs. "Now, who's the fatalist?"

Sandra draws forty D-Marks from her small wallet. "In life, Professor, there are two sides to every story and a plentitude of contradictions. So please, enjoy your Bear Paws."

The sky is a brilliant blue and cloudless outside the market, and the snow on the sidewalks has begun to melt. As they part ways, Sandra waves goodbye and blows him a kiss.

IN EARLY JANUARY, the disheartening news continues.

We are barely two weeks into the New Year, and yesterday will be recorded as another day of carnage and mourning on our calendars. Already referred to as "Black Friday," eight people were killed and 20 wounded by a single mortar round as they waited in line to collect water at the brewery. The Bosnian-Serb Army claims that the shelling was the work of Bosnian forces to paint the Serbs as inhumane. The Bosnian army denies this accusation and points the finger back at the JNA.

"It's relentless," Jusuf mutters and listens carefully to the casualties' names, his greatest fear being that he'll hear the name Sandra Fazlic. He's relieved that no one he knows has been killed. The local news follows. Forty-five residents of the last functioning convalescent home have recently died from the cold, information which only adds insult to injury. Jusuf's anxieties blot out the reports that President Bush and President Yeltsin have signed Start II, the second Strategic Arms Reduction Treaty, and the space shuttle Endeavor has rocketed into space for the third time.

As he regains his focus, the newscaster completes her report.

As of today, January 15th, 1993, this 285th day of the siege, 1,940 Sarajavaen civilians have been killed or are missing. That's called urbicide, a term defined as a deliberate attempt to destroy our beloved city, not to mention our Sarajevo soul. What's more, close to 1.2 million Bosnians have been displaced from their homes. That's 20,000 new refugees every day, and that's now described as ethnic cleansing.

Urbicide? Ethnic Cleansing? Just when you think it can't get worse, it seems to. The atrocities become more inhumane with every passing day. But, until tomorrow, this is Lana Ulak for Radio Sarajevo 202, urging you to be careful and safe, with the hope that you can find a little joy in your life.

Jusuf moves from the kitchen table and sits at the piano. He rests his head on the fallboard and reaches down to stroke Dzukela's ears. His helplessness to stem the tide of killing and ethnic cleansing fills him with shame and a sense of guilt. The media frequently refers to his fellow Bosniaks as "the heroic people of Sarajevo." He wonders if he's truly one of them. What has he done that's heroic? He thinks of Salomon Smolianoff, the master Jewish counterfeiter who survived German death camps by forging British banknotes while his relatives were gassed. Is tutoring General Ilic's daughter selling out like Smolianoff? She's only eleven, for God's sake, and her father, before the siege began and he left Sarajevo to serve in the Bosnian-Serb army, was a very good friend. And maybe still is. Jusuf wonders, at one point or another, doesn't everyone do something to stay alive? Isn't this the type of trade-off—large or small—that people make every day? Does doing his best to survive make him better or worse than the others?

He slams his hands on the fallboard and stands. "Let's go, Dzukela. We're going for water to show the bastards we're not afraid."

SANDRA STANDS WITH HER BACK against an abandoned shipping container when Jusuf arrives at the spot where he crosses the Dragon of Bosnia Street. "Oh, thank God, you're alive," she says. "When I didn't hear your name on the list, I hoped you'd be here today."

"And me you."

"Another bullet dodged." She smiles. "Or not fired. No matter, I'd like an escort to the brewery."

"Gladly," Jusuf says and reaches for her hand. "Let's hope our good fortune continues."

At the entrance to the brewery, Jusuf searches for Emir's friend. When he can't locate him, he asks the soldier on duty if it's Aron Vidic's time to be with his family.

The guard looks down at his boots and then up at Jusuf. "Are you a friend of Sergeant Vidic's?"

Jusuf says that Aron was a friend of his son.

"I'm sorry, sir," the soldier says, "but Aron was our lone casualty in yesterday's attack."

Jusuf draws an audible breath. "What a waste. What another senseless waste. How does a young man like you make sense of all this?"

"We're trained to play the odds, sir, that only one in five will die. Unfortunately, all of us know a number of the unlucky 'ones.'"

Sandra moves her hand in a circle on Jusuf's back to comfort him. "I'm so sorry. Perhaps a cry would do you good."

BURDENED WITH FULL WATER BOTTLES, they cross the Miljaka before Jusuf speaks again. "Yes, a cry might help, but these are wounds of the mind as well as the heart."

"And only someone like you can separate them," Sandra says.

Jusuf sighs. "Someone old and tired like me?"

"No, someone who's seen a lot. A Partisan who fought the Nazis. A caring person who views himself, first and foremost, as a Bosnian. A Sarajevan. An artist who is—"

"Naïve," Jusuf interrupts. "Unrealistically optimistic about the kindness of the human spirit, of mankind's innate intelligence. And all of this just to right the wrongs of a 600-year-old myth that teaches that all Muslims should be purged from the Serbian people? And because that Serbian bastard Milosevic's political power grabs are cloaked as struggles for independence? Whatever happened to our old piety of 'Brotherhood and Unity'? Has it been abandoned forever? Help me understand, Sandra. Please help me understand."

"You don't need help, Jusuf. Not you, of all people. All you need is faith and patience. Rare commodities these days, I know." She pulls his arm close to her. "It's easy for me to lecture someone else, but it's the best advice I can give."

Jusuf nods. "On my good days, I know you're right. But truthfully, don't you miss the days when we were intertwined peacefully? When mosques, synagogues, and churches stood side by side? When we all drank coffee together, and people didn't think about who was who?"

"Of course I do," Sandra says. "So, be patient. In time, the 'Bosnian Spirit' will prevail."

"You promise?"

"If you promise not to abandon your beliefs."

JUSUF SETS THE FULL BOTTLES on the kitchen table and smiles at his daughter-in-law. "Water, water, everywhere, and now a drop to drink."

"Great," Leila says and moves close to Jusuf and lowers her voice. "You seem so happy when you return from your trips for water or the Markale. You're like a schoolboy. Are you seeing someone?"

"At my age?"

Leila smiles. "Is that a 'yes' or a 'no'?"

"That's a silly question."

"I'll take that as a 'yes.'" She embraces her father-in-law and says she'll never raise it again unless he wants to talk about it, but the idea makes her very happy.

Jusuf switches on the radio. As he's learned to expect, the news is worse than the day before.

Fighting in the Croat-Bosnian war—the war within a war—has spread down the Lasva Valley. Yesterday, under Commander Dario Kordic, mortar fire and snipers massacred one hundred and three Bosnian civilians in Ahmici in what Kordic refers to as "a little light housekeeping." What's more, the mosque was burned to the ground, and its minaret demolished. At this point, discussions to restore the alliance between the two factions have been tabled.

Now for an important item from America. Susan Sontag, the writer, filmmaker, philosopher, and political activist, has come here on what skeptics have described as a "war safari," meaning that she was here for a quick look at how those of us on the reservation live and will be gone in a matter of hours. But Ms. Sontag plans to return in July and put on a play to show the world that Sarajevo remains as modern and sophisticated as any civilized city. The play is Samuel Beckett's Waiting for Godot. It's a brilliant choice for all of us who are waiting for President Clinton and the rest of the world to wake up, waiting for our deliverance.

And a helpful alert from the Jewish Community Center: the family of an octogenarian who hoarded his medications has posthumously donated a large supply of the water pill hydrochlorothiazide.

Wrapping up April 17, 1993, the 375th day of the siege, 1,508 Sarajevan civilians have been killed or reported missing, and more than 1.3 million Bosnians have been displaced from their homes. Until tomorrow, this is Lana Ulak for Radio Sarajevo 202, urging you to be careful and safe and find a little joy in your life.

Jusuf stares at the small transistor radio in disbelief. The massacre in Ahmici tells him that his family wouldn't have been as safe in Zagreb as he'd hoped. He lifts Dzukela to his lap and says, "A stroke of good fortune, little one, but right now, if I hurry, I might get some pills for my heart."

⬯

AS HE APPROACHES THE OLD SYNAGOGUE, he's surprised to find Milan following him. "I'm here for blood pressure medicine," Jusuf says. "And you?"

"The same," Milan says.

"Well, at least we still have that in common."

Milan shrugs and looks away.

At the desk where the no-longer-needed items are being doled out, Jusuf asks if the diuretics he'd heard about on the radio are still available.

The woman behind the desk looks up and smiles. "Why, Professor Kurtovic. How nice to see you. I only wish the Philharmonic was still performing. It would make this horrible situation more tolerable. And, yes, you're in luck; we still have the water pills; two bottles of ninety tablets each."

"Hold on," Milan says. "Just because he got here first doesn't mean he can have them all."

"I'm sorry, sir, but our distribution policy is on a first-come-first-served basis," the woman says. "It keeps arguments to a minimum."

"It's okay," Jusuf says. "One bottle for me and one for Mr. Radic."

The woman hands Milan a bottle, and he hurries to leave.

Jusuf calls after him. "Aren't you forgetting something?"

Milan stops short of the exit. "Of course. Thank you, Jusuf. Thank you very much."

Jusuf smiles. "You owe me one."

Milan dismisses him with a wave of his hand and pushes open the heavy door.

The woman looks at Jusuf. "That was very thoughtful of you, Professor. Do you know Mr. Radic well?"

"He lives close by and, at one time, was a friend," Jusuf says. "I don't know what to call him now, and I don't think he knows either."

JUSUF HAS TAKEN DZUKELA for his brief morning walk before Leila and her daughters join him at the kitchen table. "I've got a treat for you," he says. "A very special treat."

"Oh, goodie," Ema says. "Orange juice, scrambled eggs, and sour cream!"

Jusuf smiles but shakes his head.

"Okay, let me guess," Irma says. "Fresh white bread roll with Nutella and Kras Express cocoa?"

Jusuf chuckles. "I'm afraid I can't offer you food for your stomachs, but I can offer you food for your minds and your souls. The American writer Susan Sontag is putting on *Waiting for Godot* tonight at Pozoriste mladih, and I have four tickets. And only a hundred can go because it will be lighted by candlelight."

"Do I have to go?" Ema asks. "Won't I be bored?"

"Yes, you have to go," her mother says. "And, no, I don't think you'll be bored." She turns to Jusuf. "Will Sontag be there?"

"I would think so. It was her idea, and she's directing it. Not only that, she's the first celebrity to denounce the siege publicly as genocide." He smiles at his granddaughters. "So far, so good?"

Their mother answers for them: "Better than good; it's a brilliant treat."

Jusuf is delighted that his family will join him to watch what he considers an important performance. But, he's confused by leading a life that he thinks is filled with so many contradictions. Leila no longer goes to the Markale and rarely visits her friends in the neighborhood. The teenagers' only trips are to their schooling places. Yet here they are, all going to the theater, as though they don't have a care in the world.

Jusuf quietly says a prayer that he's doing the right thing.

SUSAN SONTAG WAVES GOODBYE to the appreciative viewers as they file out of the Pozoriste mladih. Once outside, Jusuf waits for one of his family members to volunteer her impression. He's startled when it is Ema who speaks first. "Dedo, that was so good. It's about us, right? We're like her Didi and Gogo, waiting for someone to show up who never does. How cool is that?"

"Way cool," Irma says.

Jusuf is pleased that the play's significance is not lost on his teenagers. "Right," he says. "But, let's hope our real-life play doesn't end that way."

A man near them stops and turns to face them. "Don't listen to your grandfather, young lady. Nobody is coming for you."

"My word, Milan, you seem to be everywhere," Jusuf says. "It's almost as though you're keeping an eye on us."

Milan smiles and shakes his head.

Ema looks to her grandfather. "Do you think Mr. Radic is right, Dedo? That no one will ever help us? Not even the United States?"

Before Jusuf can answer, Milan says, "If anyone were going to help you, they would have intervened long ago. It's not America's war, Ema. Please understand, they don't want any part of it. So, tell your grandfather to take my advice and get out of Bosnia if he can. Go to Germany, or even better, the US. You'll see. Karadzic is planning on crushing you in the coming months."

"Whose side are you on anyway, Mr. Radic?" Ema asks.

"Neither. I'm caught in the middle," Milan says and wishes them a good night.

Jusuf takes Ema by the arm. "Let's go home and talk about the play before the shelling starts again. I'm just glad you enjoyed the play."

"But," Ema says, "Mr. Radic has always been so nice to us. What's changed?"

"This war is confusing a lot of Serbs, not just Milan," Jusuf says. "That's what's changed."

IRMA AND EMA EMERGE from the cellar and huddle around the woodstove, their down jackets zipped to their throats. Jusuf greets them with his usual "good morning, ladies," and asks if they slept well. Irma blows on her hands to warm them. "I could have used another blanket but was too lazy to get up and grab one from the pile."

Ema says she's starved.

"Well, you're in luck," their grandfather says. "Thanks to a UN drop, we have powdered eggs, biscuits, and half a cup of coffee each."

"Oh, goody," Irma giggles. "More biscuits from the Vietnam war. What's the date of this batch? Nineteen-seventy?"

Jusuf laughs. "Nineteen sixty-seven, but they're high in protein."

"Or were," Irma says.

"No matter," Leila says. "Don't look a gift horse in the mouth."

"Really, Mom, a gift horse?" Ema asks.

Leila smiles. "One of your grandmother's favorite expressions."

"One of her many," Jusuf says and asks the girls what their school itinerary is for the day.

"We're on the 10:00 to 2:00 schedule at the apartment building on Saraci Street," Irma says.

"And we've got our friends and our Dedo and our Dzukela right here," Ema adds. "Much better than if we'd gone to stay with our cousins. How's that for not looking a gift horse in the mouth?"

"Perfect," her mother says. "Keep on being positive, and don't give up. Someone will eventually save us. Someone will have to. Morals will overcome political posturing."

"So, we're not like waiting for Godot?" Ema asks.

"That's the hope," Leila says. "That's the hope."

AFTER THE GIRLS LEAVE for school, Leila says that while Jusuf practices, she'd like to get out of the house for a change of scenery and visit her friend Maja who's just had a baby.

"Maja Demir?" Jusuf exclaims. "Another baby? At her age? Good for her but, please, be careful."

Leila assures him that she'll be okay, that it's a safe walk to Maja's house.

Once he finishes his coffee, he sorts through the reams of paper in the piano bench. He settles on Bartok's concerto number three. He sits at the piano and studies the solo passages to refresh his memory. He loves the light, airy nature of the piece and looks forward to playing it to amuse himself. He draws a deep breath, pauses, and begins to play the first delicate notes when there is a loud banging on his door and his enthusiasm for playing leaves him. He's surprised that someone is paying him a call, something that has happened infrequently since the siege began. Milan reaches for him and grabs him by his arms when he opens the door. "Leila has been wounded. Come quickly."

As they run up Logavina Steet, Jusuf asks, "Is she badly hurt?"

"I'm so sorry. I have no idea where the sniper was hiding."

Jusuf feels as though he's running in quicksand. Try as he might, he doesn't seem to be getting any closer. He asks again if Leila has been badly hurt, although he's not sure he wants to hear the truth.

"Yes, she's badly hurt," Milan says.

Jusuf thinks she has to be alright, that he can't lose Emir and Leila, too. That simply could not happen. To the girls. To him. He searches for Leila in the small crowd that has gathered when he and Milan arrive. His neighbors look away when he makes eye contact with them. Someone has already drawn a sheet over Leila near the intersection where she was shot. "Oh my God!" he shouts. "She's dead?"

"Sorry, Jusuf," Milan says. "I didn't know how to tell you."

Jusuf pulls back the sheet to look at his daughter-in-law. Her temple shows a single, almost surgical wound. "First Emir, now this," he says. Bile fills his throat, and for an instant, he struggles to maintain his balance. Oddly, he feels as though he's a distant bystander, void of emotion. Thoughts come and go slowly, and images seem to be in black and white. His heart races. He tries to get his bearings and steady himself by drawing deep breaths. It doesn't help. He stares at Leila and thinks how beautiful she was on her wedding day, how happy she'd made Sara and him, how much Emir loved her. His disbelief and horror are of little consequence, and he collapses on all fours. Milan reaches to steady him and says, "I told you that you should leave."

Jusuf gently brushes Milan's hand from his shoulder and leans forward to kiss Leila's forehead. He begins to cry and lowers himself to gently cover her as though he's protecting her from further harm. He whispers, "I'll take care of them. As God is my witness, I will."

He stands slowly and looks at Leila's friend Maja, who heaves with sobs while holding her infant close to her. "What do I tell the girls, Maja?" he asks. "How in God's name will I ever explain this? Comfort them?"

Maja says, "I'll do whatever I can to help, but right now I can't think about anything except how much I'll miss her."

Jusuf turns to Milan. "What more? I don't think I can stand any more."

Milan shrugs and looks away.

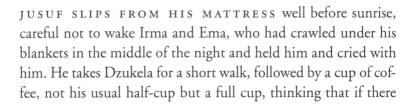

JUSUF SLIPS FROM HIS MATTRESS well before sunrise, careful not to wake Irma and Ema, who had crawled under his blankets in the middle of the night and held him and cried with him. He takes Dzukela for a short walk, followed by a cup of coffee, not his usual half-cup but a full cup, thinking that if there ever was a time that he could justify pampering himself, this was it. He's already arranged to have Leila bathed and wrapped in white linen and delivered to the nearby Vrbanjusa cemetery where she will be buried next to the empty grave he's reserved as a memorial to Emir, a grave that he begrudgingly accepts will remain empty forever.

He sits at the kitchen table and struggles to make sense of his predicament. He realizes he's at a crossroads, that he faces the most difficult decisions of his life. As of yesterday, his two bewildered granddaughters are no longer a shared responsibility; they've been orphaned by this pointless war and are his charges. His alone. He must decide what's best for them and leave his feelings out of it. He scolds himself once again that he must take life one day at a time, no matter what. Live in the present. Stick with the comfort of familiar routines. Do anything that gives him boundaries.

∞

WEEKS PASS, weeks filled with tears and sleepless nights. Irma has become almost mute. Ema has begun to smoke and her skin has broken out in a rash. Jusuf jams his hands into the pockets of his baggy pants and lowers his gaze to the floor before facing his granddaughters. They huddle by the warmth of the woodstove and nervously glance at each other. Finally, Irma asks if there's something wrong.

"Yes and no, but I want to talk with the two of you, and you must understand that all I want is what's best for you." He forces a smile in an attempt to relieve the girls' apprehension. And his. They give each other a puzzled look but nod. "It's simply this: it isn't wise for you to remain in Sarajevo any longer. Even the Chetniks are telling our women and children to leave. And you've seen what can happen in the blink of an eye to someone you love."

"What are you trying to tell us, Dedo?" Irma asks.

"What I'm trying to say is I think you should go someplace safe until the war is over. Someplace where you'd have a family who loves you. Without your mother. . . . " He fails to finish his thought. "There are organizations in America that arrange homes for kids like you, and I've explored how it works and if it would be right for you."

"We'd go to America?" Ema says. "No way, Dedo, no way."

Jusuf sighs. "It's what's best for you. With no end of the war in sight, if you stay, you'll live in constant danger with little or no food, poor schooling, very few friends, and no way to enjoy life and relax. You'll be deprived of enjoying your teenage years and your education, something I don't want to happen."

"You can't do this to us, Dedo," Ema says. "It's not fair."

Jusuf's voice rises, something that his granddaughters have never heard before. "For God's sake, Ema, think about it. First, your father and now your mother. And there are reports of young girls being raped in front of their fathers. What more evidence do you need?" He reaches for Ema's hand. "Sorry to be so stern, but in America you'll be safe without all the constant worries, both your worries and mine. Yes, mine. Every time I hear a bomb explode when you're not with me, I think the worst. And if you stay and something happens to me, what then? Who will look after you? I know this is a huge surprise and a lot to consider, but I've arranged for permits for you to leave as soon as possible."

Irma says she needs time to think about it and asks if they have a choice, if they can say no.

"I hope that when you've talked it over, you'll agree it's best for you."

Ema begins to sob. "Will you come with us?"

"What a sweet question, but the answer is no. And, please, don't worry about me. I'll remain here with my students, in my house, with Dzukela, and I promise that I'll stay safe. It may be hard for you to understand, but I want Sarajevo to be the last stop on my journey. Hopefully, you'll come back to me when the war is over."

Irma wraps an arm around her sister's shoulder and pulls her close to her. "We should talk, Ema. Think this through. I'm already dreaming about finding a place to heal, about soft beds, hot showers, and cheeseburgers."

∽

"KURTOVIC," the military policeman barks, breaking the static on his field telephone. "Kurtovic, Irma. Kurtovic, Ema."

The girls are crouched in the dark with Jusuf, waiting to escape through the Sarajevski tunel—The Tunnel of Hope—to the UN free territory of Butmir and on to America and the chance of a new life. Jusuf looks at his watch, the luminous dial washing a green glow on his white beard, his tear-filled eyes hidden in the shadow of his heavy brows. He pulls his granddaughters against him, the wetness of their eyes and mouths warm against him.

There is a whistling sound, then an explosion and the winter night is lit by a flare dangling bright white beneath a miniature parachute as it drifts above the countryside. "Down!" yells the MP, and Jusuf pushes the girls to the snow-covered ground and shields them with his body.

The flare descends silently, illuminating leafless trees and the remains of pockmarked cinderblock buildings. For a moment, it lights the airstrip, then slips behind a burnt-out high-rise, its hollow windows gaping like the eyes, nose, and mouth of a gray jack-o-lantern, and all are wrapped in darkness once again.

"Now!" the MP says.

Jusuf helps the girls to their feet, presses them against his chest for the last time, and leads them toward the guard.

"No," Ema cries. "Please, Dedo, can't I stay? Please."

"This is no place for girls like you," Jusuf says.

Ema begins to cry. "But I'll miss you, Dedo. I love you so much. Please, please, please come with us."

"I would if I could." Jusuf wraps his arms around her once again. "I love you, too, and Irma. More than you'll ever know. But in times like these, everyone must do whatever they can to make life better, and I'm needed here." He reaches for Irma and embraces both girls as tears run down his cheeks. He lets go of his granddaughters and steps back to look at them. Their caring and their loyalty make him proud of them. Yet, their fear of the unknown makes separating difficult. So very difficult. He forces a smile. "Not to worry, I'll take the best of care of Dzukela. Maybe now he'll sleep on *my* bed."

"Welcome to Sarajevo's metro," the MP says and hands the girls their papers and cotton masks. "I'm afraid there's lots of water tonight. The pumps aren't working, and the air quality is very poor." He takes them by the arms of their thick parkas and winks at them. "Watch your heads and come back to me."

The girls pick their way down the steep wood steps into the tunnel. From the hills, they hear the familiar *pop pop pop* of snipers firing at those who are trying to flee by running across the airport runway, and they hear their grandfather's voice one last time. "Careful, Ema. Listen to Irma. This is the only way. And for God's sake, be safe, and write often."

Ema stops and turns to catch one last look at her Dedo. Irma places a hand on her backpack and nudges her forward. "Move, Ema. You'll hold up the others."

"I don't care," Ema says. As she stoops to enter the tunnel, the top of her backpack catches on a wood beam overhead. She bends further and takes another step, the icy water now sloshing above her knees. The smell of mud and stagnant water engulf her. She steps again, and the toe of her boot catches on something hard and immovable. She pitches forward, an electric cable brushing her face, the yellow bulb that hangs from it swinging and throwing shadows across the steel walls. A rat races along a narrow black pipe, past the crouched, ghost-like forms of the people in front of her. She steadies herself and stops. "Oh, my God, Irma, please help me. I don't want to do this." She tries to turn to face her sister, but the tunnel is too narrow, no wider than her shoulders. She hunches over, her hands on her knees like a winded athlete, with the weight of her backpack and all her earthly belongings pressing heavily on her. She begins to cry again.

"Go, little sister," Irma says and pats her pack to comfort her, not to hurry her. "There's no turning back."

The sisters endure two frigid hours of starting, stopping, stumbling, and waiting as they slosh the half-mile to the UN free territory of Butmir. Another parachute flare ignites overhead at the tunnel's exit, and they drop to their denim-clad knees. The sky behind them now glows the familiar "Sarajevo red" from fires and tracer shells. Heavy shelling and sniper fire force them to crawl in a trench that leads across an open field, the cold of the snow burning their knees and hands. As they begin to crawl, Irma grabs Ema's sodden pant leg and points toward a small crudely lettered sign: **Paris 3,765 km**. "See, Ema," she whispers, "soon we'll be free."

"And away from all that I love."

"Loved," Irma says. "Our city, our parents, our school, they're all gone."

"What about our Dedo and our Dzukela?"

"When the war's over, we'll go back to them."

"You sure?" Ema asks.

"I'm positive."

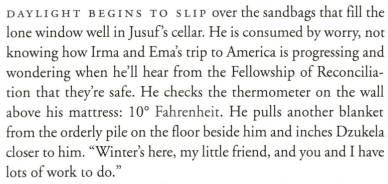

DAYLIGHT BEGINS TO SLIP over the sandbags that fill the lone window well in Jusuf's cellar. He is consumed by worry, not knowing how Irma and Ema's trip to America is progressing and wondering when he'll hear from the Fellowship of Reconciliation that they're safe. He checks the thermometer on the wall above his mattress: 10° Fahrenheit. He pulls another blanket from the orderly pile on the floor beside him and inches Dzukela closer to him. "Winter's here, my little friend, and you and I have lots of work to do."

Warmed by his carefully-chosen nightclothes (wool socks, loose-fitting sweatpants, a frayed sweatshirt, and a black watch cap which he'll add to as the temperature drops), he rushes to the bathroom—dubbed "Siberia" by his granddaughters—then hurries up the stairs to light the woodstove. Snow has fallen overnight, and the view from the kitchen window brings a smile to his face. He thinks the skiing would be great at the Olympic mountain if only . . . He sighs and pours a few drops of kerosene on a small log and sets a match to it. While he waits for the stove to heat the cup filled with the remains of the coffee from the day before, he dutifully takes his diuretic and eats two slices of bread with a spread of powdered milk, oil, and yeast.

Once he completes his morning routine, he remains at the kitchen table to prioritize his lonely daily activities. It's a process that demands far more discipline than it has in the past. Since the siege began, he thinks there have been so damn many distractions and worries, and while he doesn't think he's becoming senile, thoughts do seem to pass through his mind before he can hold them in place. Nonetheless, he thinks it's time to prepare for winter's harshness and commits to approaching things as efficiently as possible, reminding himself that, if he's going to see this war to its end, at sixty-eight he must conserve his energy and strength. He begins by making a list of the students he has committed to teach in the coming year. He shakes the ballpoint pen that every few words shows signs of running out of ink and scribbles a reminder to find more sandbags for the ground floor windows.

He stands, stretches his arms and back, and says, "What have I forgotten?" He laughs at how much he talks to himself and Dzukela since Irma and Ema left him but admits that laughing is a release he enjoys. "And what the hell, who can hear me anyway? It's now my life to screw up as I please. I'm on my own."

He trudges upstairs with a broom and dustpan in hand and peers into each of the three small bedrooms. All the mattresses had been taken from their bed frames and moved to the basement on the siege's second day, and many of the bureau drawers gape open. Jusuf sweeps up the glass fragments from the windows that the shelling has shattered, draws the shades, and collects a few unwanted articles of clothing that hang in the closets. As he shuts each door, he makes a mental note of the furniture that can be sawed into firewood, reserving a few bureau drawers to use as planters for small vegetable gardens when, and if, he lives long enough to enjoy another spring.

At the foot of the stairs, he looks out the window that over-looks Logavina Street. Milan is standing on the sidewalk, staring at his house. Jusuf opens the window and calls to him. "I took your advice and sent the girls to America."

Milan shakes his head. "Your family minus your only child and his wife."

Jusuf bites his lip and nods.

"And for what?" Milan asks. "Some misguided sense of patriotism? A clever man like you should have known better before all this started. What were you thinking, Professor? Whatever it was, you were so wrong, and you may well pay for your stubbornness. I only hope I'm wrong."

Jusuf closes the window and watches as Milan turns on his heel and starts down the street. Jusuf wonders how he lived alongside neighbors like him and didn't know. He feeds several slivers of wood into the stove, warms his hands, and sits at the piano to settle his nerves. Soon Brahms' second piano concerto fills every corner of his vacant house. Searching for sandbags will have to wait.

∞

A MONTH AFTER IRMA AND EMA arrive in America, a young woman who works in the local Associated Press office delivers a letter from them. Jusuf settles in his favorite chair near the woodstove and opens their long-awaited news, hoping that they are happy and well, that he has done the right thing.

November 8, 1993
Number 1
Dear Dedo!

Here we are, safely, in Haverford, Pennsylvania! WOW!! Can you believe it? It's a relief and weird and a bit scary. Mr. Barnes thinks it's a good idea to number our letters to make it easier for you to keep track of them because getting mail to you will be unpredictable. He has contacts at the AP and the Philadelphia Inquirer and will run off copies at his law office to give their journalists when they travel to Sarajevo. So fingers crossed! Let's hope you get this.

The trip took a lot longer than we were told it would. Our contact in Butmir drove us for what seemed like forever, bouncing around in the bed of his truck under a smelly canvas cover!

The Fellowship of Reconciliation woman who met us at the Budapest airport made us change into our best clothes and taught us about travel-ing on an airplane. I was a little scared on the flight to London, but Ema loved it, even the bumpy parts. In London, a Bosnian woman who worked for British Airways "upgraded" us to business class, and we were treated like little queens all the way to Philadelphia. We ate almost everything on the menu and watched two movies !!!

Mr. and Mrs. Barnes, our host family, are very friendly and are trying hard to make us feel wel-come. And they live in a mansion! Ema says they're kind of weird because they keep their napkins in silver rings and call each other 'thee' and 'thou.' But they explained that's the way Quakers, people of their beliefs, address each other.

When we showed them pictures of you and Mom and Dad and Dzeukela, Mrs. Barnes said you were lovely-looking people. Mr. Barnes knew everyone's name. He even called you the Professor. And they were very gentle when they mentioned Mom and Dad's deaths.

We each have our own bedroom with super comfortable beds and our own bathroom. AND WE CAN TAKE AS MANY HOT SHOWERS AS WE LIKE! It's complete luxury, and our hosts even let their German Shepherd sleep on Ema's bed to comfort her.

That's all for now. We'll write again soon when we have more to report. So please don't worry about us; we're safe and, as you can see, comfortable and still spinning from the newness of it all.

We miss how your music always filled our house and pray for your safety every night.

Give Dzukela a big cuddle from both of us.
With all the love in the world,
Irma and Ema
P.S. We'll come back to you, Dedo. Irma promised.
—Ema

ON THE DAY BEFORE THE NEW YEAR, long after the sun has begun to brighten the frigid morning, Jusuf sits at his piano, sipping a small coffee, lost in thought. He's waiting for the stove to warm his hands enough to play. He knows that a

New Year's Eve during the siege will be very different from those he's celebrated in the past. The well-lighted streets once crowded with tourists from Croatia, Serbia, and Montenegro will be dark and threatening, inhabited only by the shadowy forms of stray dogs and thieves as they move silently in search of their prey. The traditionally busy markets and malls will be empty, the popular performances in the Bascarsija silenced. The elegant parties in hotels, restaurants and private clubs will be canceled with the hope that they'll be celebrating next year's Docek Nove Godine in a grand fashion. What dispirits him most is that he and his fellow musicians will not perform one of the high points of their calendar, the Philharmonic's traditional New Year's Eve concert.

He rubs his hands together and stretches his fingers, and wonders for what seems the thousandth time how long this damn war will last. And will his heart be strong enough for him to live through it? And will the Philharmonic survive?

Perhaps unconsciously seeking a New Year's resolution, he tries to figure out where he fits in the scheme of things. He's been so preoccupied with the loss of Emir and Leila and the girls moving to America—and, yes, by merely trying to survive—that he hasn't given much else any thought. He looks at Dzukela curled at his feet next to the piano pedals and says, "What I do know, little one, is that I'm alive, a living, breathing human being. And I'm a musician, a pianist. And I'm all by myself, and I've got to figure out what all that means." He stares at the keyboard as though he is waiting for it to give him guidance. Then, slowly and with great emotion, he plays Beethoven's *Moonlight* Sonata.

When he's finished, he places his half-full cup on the stove. While he waits for the dregs of his coffee to warm, he looks out one of the few windows that has survived the shelling and stares at the pile of rocky rubble that once had been his next-door neighbor's home. He shakes his head in disgust. They were a happily married Serb and Croat couple who called the Bosnian Army *their* Army and cheered for them, dear friends to his entire family who never gave up hope, and they'd been driven from Sarajevo in a humanitarian convoy. And for what?

Mid-afternoon, Jusuf sits by the stove bundled in his down jacket and wool cap, with Dzukela curled in his lap. He is re-reading *Don Quixote,* wondering if he too isn't losing his mind like the man from La Mancha.

As the afternoon slowly turns to night, he lights a candle and continues to read until he can no longer see the print without straining. He feeds Dzukela, heats a German frankfurter, cuts a small slice of bread, and slowly eats his dinner. When he's finished, he returns to the piano to practice in blackness, a routine that hones his skills and one that he encourages his students to adopt. "However, it's a bigger lesson than just learning how to play without looking at the keys," he tells them. "It will also teach you how to make the best of a bad situation, something that should hold you in good stead throughout your life, no matter what you pursue."

Once satisfied that he's practiced enough for the day, he zips his parka, knots a wool scarf at his throat, and leashes his little companion for their hurried nightly walk. He follows his familiar route, never straying far from Logavina Street. He enjoys the autonomy of walking the streets lit only by the moon and an occasional sliver of light escaping from behind a boarded-up window. There are prolonged moments of silence during the lulls in the distant shelling, other than the crunching sound of his boots in the snow. However, Jusuf thinks that things are never wholly silent because he can still hear the city's heart—the courage of the Bosnian people—continuing to beat. He kicks at the snow and sighs. It's thoughts like this that make him wonder if he hasn't gone over the edge like Don Quixote, that the war is damaging him in ways he can't identify. He worries that he's becoming a mystery to himself.

Ahead of him, standing in the night's darkest shadows, a man smokes a cigarette, its glow illuminating his heavy face. As Jusuf approaches him, Milan steps onto the sidewalk, blocking his path. "Violating the curfew again, Professor?"

Jusuf forces a smile. "Why, no, Milan, I'm just celebrating New Year's Eve."

"Well, I can assure you that it won't be a happy one for you if you don't play by the rules."

Jusuf checks the luminous dial on his watch. "But it's only a little after eight. I've got another hour until the curfew begins."

"I don't think you get it," Milan says. "If you weren't tutoring Colonel Ilic's daughter, you'd have been driven from your home long ago." He steps back into the dark and gestures for Jusuf to continue on his way.

As he heads for home, Jusuf hears Milan's parting warning: "You're living on borrowed time, Professor. Please don't do anything to fuck it up."

Borrowed time? Don't fuck it up? Try as he might, Jusuf can't dismiss these words or erase them from his mind. All he can do to neutralize them is live in the present as fully as he knows how and fight the temptation to succumb to the undertow of hopelessness.

That will be his New Year's resolution.

LATER IN JANUARY, the same young woman from the AP delivers another letter from Irma and Ema.

November 16, 1993
#2

Dear Dedo—

We waited a week before writing again to be sure we had lots to tell you. And we do!

Our new school is called Shipley and has a big, beautiful campus. It's half boys and girls, and Mr. Barnes says it's the best school on the Main Line (we still don't know what 'Main Line' means). I'm in the tenth grade, and Ema is in seventh until they know more about where we belong. So far, the teachers are very helpful, and the kids are super friendly. Our teachers asked everyone to imagine how hard it must be for us not to think about what is going on in Sarajevo when we know that our friends and family were being bombed at that very moment. With that, the kids had so many questions that we had spent all our free time answering them.

Over the weekend, Mrs. Barnes took us shopping at a huge mall in a town called King of Prussia. (Wasn't that Frederick the Great? No one here seems to know.) It took quite a while to get used to not having a UN policeman or UN 4Runner at every intersection. The mall had every store and product you've ever heard of, and Ema and I agreed that nothing here has been affected by our nightmare in Bosnia.

Maybe we're a little bit jealous, or it's all just too new for us. Still, as much fun as we had buying clothes for school (plus a pair of Levi 501s each!), it makes us feel guilty about being here. We're beginning to understand why some say those who got out of Bosnia are more traumatized than those who stayed.

Mrs. Barnes is amazed at all the little things we have been deprived of. She's made appointments with her dentist to get our teeth cleaned and checked and with her gynecologist and bought an ointment for skin allergies because Ema has broken out the way she did after Dad and Mom's deaths. And one last thing, Mrs. Barnes has already opened bank accounts for us and promised to give us a monthly allowance of fifty dollars each. (Wow, is right!)

As you can tell, while we're very lonely at times, Mr. and Mrs. Barnes are making us as comfortable as they can. Next week, we will celebrate a holiday called Thanksgiving, which features a big meal with a turkey. Ema and I thought turkeys were for Christmas, so we'll let you know.

You'll never know how much we miss you and worry about you.
Much love from us both,
Irma

JUSUF IS ABOUT TO TAKE a break from practicing when a single explosion sends tremors through his house. He's never heard or felt anything like it and, for an instant, believes he can feel the reverberations through the keys of his piano. Surrounded by deafening sirens and honking horns, he rushes in the direction of the bombing. A man on a bicycle speeds past him, yelling, "They've bombed the Markale again! We're being slaughtered like fucking animals."

∾

THE FOLLOWING MORNING Jusuf turns on the radio, wondering how much more bad news he can absorb. An irrelevant question, he thinks. He can't rewrite the past nor predict the future. And he's the only person Irma and Ema can turn to. "So, get a grip, Kurtovic. For heaven's sake, get a grip," he says as the daily report begins.

> Just when you thought things couldn't get any worse, yesterday, at 12:37 PM, they did. In the deadliest attack during the siege, a 120-millimeter mortar shell landed in the center of the crowded Markale market, killing 68 innocent people and wounding 144 others. The Army of Republika Srpska claims that the Bosnian army shelled its own people to provoke western countries to come to their aid. Hard to believe? At this point, nothing is.
>
> So, I'll sign off prematurely from this report because I'm overwhelmed by the news that I must deliver to you today. The idea of stepping around more "Roses," those grenade craters painted blood red where someone had been killed, turns my stomach.
>
> On February 5, 1974, the 670th day of the siege, 2,756 Sarajevan civilians have been reported killed or missing, and more than 1.5 million Bosnians have been displaced from their homes. Until tomorrow, this is Lana Ulak for Radio Sarajevo 202, urging you to please be careful and safe and, somehow, find a little joy in your life.

He writes his granddaughters to assure them that he's okay, hoping he can find someone to get his note to them soon so that they won't worry too much after receiving the news of the Markale massacre if it's reported in America.

EVEN THOUGH RADIO 202 announces two weeks later that February 22nd is the first casualty-free day since the siege began, many of Jusuf's fellow musicians remain more depressed than ever by the bombing of the Markale. Their lives lack purpose. Even the battle for survival isn't purpose enough. And nothing can replace the feeling of community they shared when they played together.

But in late April, Jusuf is greeted by astonishing news when he arrives at the Academy: a gala concert to raise money for the restoration of Vijecnica has been scheduled for June 19th, and the symphony will perform Mozart's Requiem, his mass for the deceased, in the City Hall's ruins.

Jusuf is thrilled to learn that Zubin Mehta will be conducting and that the singers are all artists he holds in the highest esteem. He treats himself to a smile and thinks that perhaps this is the first signal that maybe, just maybe, someday life may return to normal.

AS HE WALKS to the charred shell of Vijecnica dressed in his tuxedo that now is two full sizes too large, Jusuf thinks it's a perfect evening for the gala. The temperature is a comfortable seventy-eight degrees, and the clear June sky is marred only by smoke and dust from an afternoon shelling. There are no mortar explosions, no staccato bursts of machine gun fire. He finds the silence comforting yet unsettling and wonders if the bearded bastards are waiting for the concert to begin to wreak havoc on the musicians, dignitaries, and the crowd gathering to listen to the music as it wafts through the blown-out windows.

Once in the old City Hall, he is ushered to a small seating area for the orchestra members who are not needed for the Requiem. He is shocked by the twisted steel, bullet-pockmarked walls, piles of rocky rubble, and shattered glass but is impressed by the effort to make this event special. Spotlights hang from the balconies in the main hall, and a tiered stage has been erected over the ashes of tons of paper, the ever-present reminder of the millions of books that had been destroyed two years before. Fifty chairs have been arranged for the audience, mostly Bosnian political leaders, top UN officials, and their wives. Television cameras have been strategically placed to broadcast the event to most of Europe and the United States.

At eight o'clock, Jusuf turns to the oboe player who sits next to him. "Okay, Elvis, say your prayers that all goes well."

His colleague smiles and pats him on the knee. "I'm all prayed out, Jusuf. I've been praying all week long."

Applause fills the remains of the great hall as Zubin Mehta and the singers file onto the stage. Maestro Mehta says how devastated he is by the damage to the once charming city of Sarajevo and how thankful all should be to the world-class artists—Jose Carreras, Ruggero Raimondi, Cecilia Gasdia, and Ildiko Kmlos—who are risking their lives and donating their time for this important event. He concludes with a comment about the awe in which he and the rest of the free world hold the Bosnian people: "We have come for you to bless us more than we to bless you."

JUSUF JOINS THE ORCHESTRA and the Cathedral Choir as they file from Vijecnica. Darkness has begun to embrace the hundreds of people who wait outside to applaud each musician. As he starts on his way home, a familiar voice calls, "Professor. Professor Kurtovic. Over here." Sandra is on her tiptoes, energetically waving, hoping to be seen in the tightly packed crowd. She works her way to join him and says, "Oh, thank God. I didn't want to miss you." She takes his hands and squeezes them. "The concert was beautiful. And for such a great cause. I was so proud to know someone on that stage."

Jusuf is surprised that knowing him gave Sandra a sense of pride but is delighted. "It's a lovely piece of music," he says, "so peaceful and powerful, as though it was never to leave our grand old building but linger there forever. A fitting end to Mozart's life."

They smile at each other without speaking. Finally, Sandra asks if Jusuf would see her home. As they walk down the once-bustling main street of the old bazaar, its colorful shops and popular restaurants are now shuttered. "Do you think the Serbs didn't bomb the concert in respect of the Requiem and its Christian roots?" she asks.

Jusuf shakes his head. "An interesting theory, but I'm afraid you give the barbarians too much credit. Perhaps they're running low on munitions. Who knows? We may get the answer before I get you home."

As they approach Sandra's neighborhood, Milan hurries to join them, calling, "Professor, Mrs. Fazlic, did you enjoy the concert?"

"Why, yes, why, of course, we enjoyed the concert and the cause it supported," Jusuf says. "Vijecnica is a part of our heritage. Mine, Milan, as well as yours. It should never have been destroyed."

"Do you agree, Mrs. Fazlic?" Milan asks.

Sandra stares at the stranger. "Of course, I agree."

"Well, enjoy the rest of your evening," Milan says and begins to walk away. After a few steps, he stops. "Life is filled with surprises. Isn't it, Mrs. Fazlic?"

Jusuf is confused and irritated by Milan acting as though he's been assigned to spy on them and insisting on addressing Sandra as Mrs. Fazlic. It seems both taunting and intimate. When they reach her house, he asks, "Do you know that man?"

"In the dark it was hard to place him. Maybe from the Serb community."

"The Serb community?"

"I thought you knew. I'm a Serb."

"But, Fazlic?" Jusuf says.

"That was my husband's name. My maiden name was Zoric. Does that change the way you feel about me?"

Jusuf smiles. "Of course not. Milan was a family friend until the shooting started."

Sandra pulls him to her and kisses him on the cheek. "The difference is, I will be your friend as long as I live."

"And me, yours."

She asks if he would like to come in.

"I'd like to." Jusuf hesitates. "But it's getting late."

Sandra laughs. "What are you rushing home to, Professor? Besides, I have a bottle of Slivovitz."

"Where in the world did you get that?"

"From one of the UN blue helmets who enjoys talking with me in French."

"Thanks for the invitation," Jusuf says, "and I hope you'll understand, but I need a bit of time by myself to mull over all that's happened tonight. It takes me longer to process life's ebb and flow than it used to."

Sandra says she understands and blows him a kiss goodnight.

The shelling resumes promptly at ten o'clock, and the siege continues.

∞

The months flip by like the frames of an early black and white movie to July the following year. Every day more than three hundred mortar shells rain down on the place Jusuf calls his home. Unexploded bombs and mines are threats to every step he takes. Hospitals are shelled during visiting hours. People gathering at funerals are targeted. Tanks carrying heavily-armed men roam the streets. Serb snipers and mercenaries from Montenegro use the old Jewish cemetery on the hill as a shooting perch as though killing Muslims is a carnival game in which one keeps score. Mounds of freshly dug graves appear wherever there's a little space—in city parks, backyards, in front of apartment buildings; even the Kosovo stadium is converted into a burial ground.

The faces of those who survive are worn and anxious. Tired and weak with hunger, all have lost a great deal of weight, some as many as fifty pounds. Many smoke to curb their hunger, while others limit themselves to two cigarettes a day to save their dwindling supplies. When forced to leave their homes to collect UN rations or water, they slink like frightened animals along the bombed-out streets.

Serb paramilitary units cut off electricity. The phone lines are dead. Without trash and garbage collection, swarms of rats and flies take over entire buildings. Gasoline is no longer available, and bullet-riddled cars line the streets.

The suicide rate sky-rockets.

Jusuf no longer feels in control and struggles to fulfill his pledge to live in the moment. His life drones on in the familiar but uncomfortable pattern it has assumed without him having any say. He thinks he is wandering on a narrow path with no end in sight. What haunts him every day is that he doesn't have any idea—any idea at all—when the siege might end and if he will live to see that happy day. Dreaming of pleasurable experiences in the future has been replaced by reflecting on joyous moments from the past. He thinks it's no wonder people have lost their minds, especially people who live by themselves like him.

He thinks he's as helpless as the UN Protection Forces who do next to nothing to protect his fellow Bosnians because the UN doesn't consider Croatia or Serbia aggressors. He wonders, who do they think they're kidding? Again and again, he realizes that he must let go of his frustration and anger and focus on what he can control. He starts with surviving: pursuing sources for his heart medication, finding enough to eat, and staying warm.

Like many other Bosnians, he reads the same magazines and books over and over for entertainment. He continues to rely on Radio 202 for information about what is happening, both within Bosnia and throughout the world. Along with his companionship with Dzukela, who rarely leaves his side and curls on his pillow every lonely night, he feels that the daily broadcasts are as crucial as bread and water for his survival. And, while he leaves the spigots on his sinks and bathtub open in case the Serbs briefly turn the water on without notice, he times his collecting water from the brewery with Sandra's routine.

Each time before writing his granddaughters, to try to connect with them in any way he can, he runs a hand across the framed photograph that rests on a shelf above the woodstove. His family is huddled in front of a small stucco house in the picture. He thinks Leila is beautiful with her broad smile and long black hair. Emir, dressed in camouflage fatigues, is tall and strong looking, his large hands dangling at his sides. To Jusuf, Emir looks exactly like him at his age. Ema's head is slightly bowed, her hair combed straight back, accentuating her widow's peak. She's wearing a red turtleneck sweater that has shrunk with washing and constant wear, causing Jusuf to smile and mutter, "Some things never change." Irma stands a bit removed from the group. Her thick brown hair curves behind her ears, framing her sharp-featured face as she stares almost challengingly at the camera with bright green eyes like her mother's.

Jusuf's many letters report on anything he thinks his granddaughters might find of interest or that would lift their spirits. In turn, he enjoys Irma's chatty nature and the humorous quips from Ema about the novelty of their experiences in America.

But, Irma's letters continually fuel his desire to understand what their lives in America are like. What kind of people are the Barneses, and why have they taken his granddaughters in? Why don't they have children of their own? What kind of man is Henry Barnes, who now performs the tasks that once were his? What kind of people keep their napkins in silver rings? Ostentatious, super-wealthy, or just old-fashioned with European backgrounds? And, what kind of people address each other as thee and thou?

At times he thinks he can imagine them, but at other times his screen goes blank. He wants them to understand—"Yes, goddamn it, fully understand"—why he sent his granddaughters to them and what he was shielding them from. He was convinced that what he did was best for them. But, on many a lonely night, he's wracked with guilt, for while sending the girls to America possibly saved their lives, at the same time he gave them to total strangers, and he wishes that he could undo all that he's done. On these nights, uncertain that he's done the right thing, tears trickle down his cheeks onto his pillow.

∞

ON A HUMID WEDNESDAY in late July, Radio Sarajevo has only one story.

This morning I have the unenviable task of reporting news of the war's most brutal episode to date. Under General Ratko Mladic's command, the Bosnian Serb Army and The Scorpions, a paramilitary unit from Serbia, killed thousands of men and boys in and around Srebrenica. The 400 Dutch peacekeepers in the so-called "UN Safe Area" failed to force the Serb forces from the region and couldn't prevent the town's capture or the massacre. What's more, the Dutch battalion witnessed the dumping of the victims' bodies in mass graves, the Serbs' clumsy attempt to hide the evidence. I know we all are waiting anxiously to learn what the international community's response will be to this atrocity. Might this finally be their wake-up call?

But, no more from me. On July 23rd, 1995, this 1,203rd day of the siege, 5,184 Sarajevan civilians have been reported killed or missing, and 1.8 million Bosnians have been displaced from their homes. Until tomorrow, this is Lana Ulak for Radio Sarajevo 202, urging you to say a prayer for the men and boys who were massacred today and for their loved ones. Once again, please be safe and try to find a little joy in your life.

Good Lord, Jusuf thinks, whatever happened to the Bosnia that was such a bright international light during the Winter Olympics? He sits at the kitchen table and dashes off a note to his granddaughters.

Dearest Irma and Ema—

A hurried letter about the worst news yet, in case the newspapers in the US haven't covered it. In the past week, the Serb Army massacred more than eight thousand men and boys in Srebrenica.

No worries here. Dzukela and I are fine, and I have a new friend who joins me on my trips to the brewery for water. I miss and love you very, very much.

Dedo

SEATED IN HIS KITCHEN, Jusuf enjoys the steady breeze that keeps the heat of the early-August afternoon at bay while he reads Tolstoy's *The Death of Ivan Ilyich.* Earlier in the year, he'd burned his collection of Cervantes for warmth and thinks if the war doesn't end before the coming winter, he'll have to sacrifice his collection of Dostoevsky and, God forbid, Tolstoy too. He is jarred from this depressing thought by someone knocking at his door.

To his surprise, Sandra stands on his front stoop. She holds a canvas tote bag overflowing with clothes and is covered from head to foot with dust. Tears streak down her chalk-stained cheeks. "Good God, what has happened?" Jusuf asks. "Come in. Please. Come in."

Once inside the house, Sandra falls to her knees. She is consumed by uncontrollable sobbing. Jusuf reaches for her, but she refuses his hand. Haltingly, she says, "I came back from the market, and my house was not there. Gone, Jusuf. Gone. Literally leveled. Just a pile of concrete and choking dust. All I could salvage is in that," she says, pointing to her bag. "I didn't know where to turn, so I came here. I'm sorry to bother you, but I'm scared and desperate. I'll leave as soon as I can pull myself together."

Jusuf takes her hands and eases her to her feet. "No bother at all. Come sit. You may stay as long as you'd like. Dzukela and I can use the company. How about a brandy to calm your nerves?"

Sandra wipes at her tears. "That would be perfect."

Jusuf fills two glasses and joins her at the kitchen table. As she settles, they agree that the siege has lasted far longer than either had imagined and have no idea what the future might bring. Neither is optimistic, and at that moment, the most comfortable thing they can do is draw upon their pasts.

To keep Sandra's mind off what she's just experienced, Jusuf describes his childhood. He says what singled him out from most children was his love for music and his training with the piano. When he turned eighteen, filled with idealism and patriotic zeal, he joined the Yugoslav Partisans led by Tito to fight against the Wehrmacht. Not long after signing up, during the Battle of Kozara, his right leg was mangled by shrapnel. He smiles at Sandra and reminds her that when they first met, she'd said he ran like a duck.

She apologizes for her failed attempt at humor, but he says there's no need for apologies. "Quite the opposite. I liked the honesty and spirit behind the comment."

He tells her that after the war, he was accepted by the Royal Academy of Music in London. When the Sarajevo Philharmonic Orchestra started up again in 1948, he auditioned for the principal pianist position. Much to his surprise, Maestro Miric appointed him principal pianist.

Shortly after joining the orchestra, he married his childhood sweetheart, the stage actress Sara Terzic. They had one child, his son Emir, although they desperately tried to have more. The trauma of four miscarriages was disheartening for them both, but oddly, brought them closer together as though they were locked in a battle against a common enemy. After thirty years of marriage, Sara died of pancreatic cancer. Shortly before she died, their son married Leila Muratovi. It was a period of extreme happiness for Sara and him because Emir and Leila quickly blessed them with two granddaughters.

From here, much of what he relates, Sandra has already heard in guarded snippets. Emir joined other volunteers to defend their country against the Army of Republica Srpska. On his second day in position, Sarajevo was engulfed in fire from an estimated 3,500 mortar rounds, and Emir was never seen or heard from again. "I'll never forget that day. Never. April 21, 1992. Radio 202 declared it the most difficult and dramatic day in Sarajevo's long history. For me, it was the worst, but its impact on Ema has been far more complicated. For her, the ambiguity of Emir's loss keeps her hopes alive, and she continues to think that somehow her father survived and will return after the siege is over."

He pauses, gives Sandra a sheepish look, and asks if he's been boring her.

"Far from it," Sandra says and finishes her brandy. "Your story is more interesting than mine, lots more interesting." She describes a comfortable and sheltered childhood. After attending the Ecole des Roches, a private boarding school in the suburbs of Paris, she returned home. In a whirlwind romance, she married Goran Fazlic, a dashing socialite who had amassed a fortune trading in oil and derivatives. "That's my whole story. Married for twenty years to one of Sarajevo's most visible citizens but couldn't have children. My husband, who'd volunteered for the Patriotic League at age fifty, was killed in the battle at the Canton Building. And now, here I am, not only a widow but homeless as well."

She pours herself another brandy. "But, I'm luckier than most. I'm alive and in one piece, and I'm here with you." She stands, sets the table, and lights a candle as though she's entertaining a guest.

They slowly eat a dinner of German sausages and a slice of black bread, but with little conversation. By the time they've finished eating, heavy rain is falling, and darkness has shrouded the house, the flickering candle their only source of light.

Sandra fills their glasses with brandy and raises hers to Jusuf's. "To celebrate."

Jusuf lifts his glass. "To the hope for peace."

Sandra taps her glass to Jusuf's and takes a long drink. "And, to us."

"To us?"

Sandra takes another drink and stands. "Yes, to us." She places her glass on the table and begins to undress.

Jusuf has no idea what she is doing, let alone what she expects of him. Before she finishes undressing, she says, "And now I'd like to step into the rain and take a shower with you and wash off all this dust before the shelling begins."

A shower? Jusuf has never given the idea a thought. He's learned how to wash his whole body with a half-liter of water: a cup to wash, then a cup to rinse. But a shower? With Sandra?

She slugs another brandy, and Jusuf expects her to cover herself. Instead, she takes off her underwear and clasps her hands behind her back. "Look. It's me, Jusuf. Sandra Fazlic, age 53, with nothing to hide."

In the flickering light of the candle, the bones in her shoulders, and her ribs, are barely visible. Jusuf tries to avoid looking at her breasts out of decency, although it makes no sense.

"Now you," she says.

Jusuf flinches. "Me?"

"Oh, Jusuf, don't take life so seriously. This is supposed to be fun. Even joyous."

"But…"

"Please," Sandra says. "For me."

Jusuf sighs, finishes his brandy, and refills his glass. He takes off his shoes and socks and turns away from Sandra. He unbuttons his shirt and takes it off, and hesitates. He fumbles with the safety pin that holds up his loose-fitting trousers and slips them and his underpants to the floor. He is embarrassed by what she will see: his loss of muscle tone, his almost skeletal arms and legs, the hair that has grown on his shoulders and his back, and his rounded belly. He draws a deep breath and, shielding his penis with both hands, turns to face Sandra. Mimicking her, but with more of an apology than a proclamation, he says, "Jusuf Kurtovic, 71. Scars, potbelly, and all."

She signals with her hands for him to uncover himself. When he does, she says, "Before the war, you must have been a very powerful man. And in this light, I don't see the scars or the potbelly. I see a very thoughtful, kind man."

Jusuf starts to cover himself again but stops as Sandra takes his hand and leads him to the back door. Once outside, she reaches around him and pulls him to her. The warmth of her body against his in the downpour comforts and excites him. He hesitates, then wraps his arms around her waist.

She looks up at him. "Our own outdoor shower." She runs her fingers back through her hair, wipes her cheeks, and cups her breasts to let the water run over them. "Doesn't it feel great?" She kisses Jusuf lightly on the lips.

"I'm not sure I can do this. It's been so long. And, well—" He stops.

"Don't worry, Jusuf. It will be beautiful." She bites his lip and kisses him with an open mouth. Jusuf feels a familiar stirring that he'd worried had been lost to him. Sandra pulls back and moves her hand over him. "Well, look what I found," she giggles. "We should do this at least once before we die."

∞

JUSUF MOVES HIS CANDLE from the phone to the kitchen table and hurriedly pens a letter he knows his granddaughters will be waiting for.

August 29, 1995
Dearest Irma and Ema-

Dzukela and I are okay! I think I reached Mrs. Barnes on the phone for a second last night and tried all day today without success. The attack at the Markale was horrible, almost as bad as the first. No one we know was killed or injured.

I'll write more later. I'm in a rush to find someone to deliver this to you.
With much love,
Dedo

Jusuf isn't sure how his girls will receive the news about Sandra and thinks it's best to introduce her slowly.

PS A friend whose house was demolished by the shelling has temporarily moved in with me. Her added company has made things better for us both.

Hoping that he's taken the right approach, he puts Dzukela on his leash and hurries in the dark, abandoned streets to the Holiday Inn in search of a journalist who will take his letter to the United States.

NO MORE THAN A MONTH after the Srebrenica massacre and less than twenty-four hours after the second shelling of the Markale market, Jusuf and Sandra sit to listen to the news as Lana Ulak summarizes what many Bosnians have waited almost four years to hear.

> This morning, August 30th, 1995, at 2:00 a.m. our time, NATO announced that sixty aircraft from Italy and the US aircraft carrier Theodore Roosevelt have begun to pound Serb positions around Sarajevo. Simultaneously, French and British artillery from the Rapid Reaction Force joined in, targeting the Lukavica barracks southwest of Sarajevo, making Operation Deliberate Force the largest NATO military action in history. The thousands of targets were picked months in advance, and the strikes are referred to as "massive." US President Clinton has been quoted as wanting to "hit them hard."
>
> Perhaps our waiting for Godot wasn't in vain after all.

RAIN BEGINS TO FALL as Jusuf returns home from the Academy after a long afternoon of tutoring and celebrating the news that NATO has started their attacks and peace may not be far away. Even though he's exhausted and malnourished, a broad smile replaces the worried frown he's worn the last four years. Sandra and his fellow Bosniaks will soon be safe, and his granddaughters will fill his house with joy. He waves a hand at the street light that once again illuminates what is left of the sidewalk of Logavina Street as though it were an old friend. The rain becomes heavier, and Jusuf begins a slow jog for home. He stumbles on the cracked concrete, clutches for the collar of his shirt as though he's going to button it against the rain, and collapses on his side. Within the hour, a neighbor discovers him drenched with rain, without any signs of life.

A small group of neighbors visits Sandra to deliver the news, but she has difficulty absorbing what she's being told. "Dead?" she says. "What do you mean dead? There hasn't been any shooting in days. Injured maybe, but not dead."

A woman explains that Jusuf didn't have any wound marks, that he appeared to have died from some other complication, perhaps a heart attack. Sandra stares blankly at her as though she's not absorbing a word she's saying. "Can I see him?"

The woman takes Sandra's hand and says the Professor is on his way to the undertaker and that she should give it a little time.

"But the burial," Sandra says. Her neighbors say they'll help with that, but she should first notify Jusuf's granddaughters.

She writes Irma and Ema a hurried note, carefully introducing herself and explaining how much she loved their grandfather and how much he loved them. And, every day the following week, she tries to reach the girls by telephone without success.

Mid-month, a messenger from the AP delivers a letter addressed to Jusuf Kurtovic.

September 1, 1995
#15
Dear Dedo—

I honestly don't know if I have the strength to write this letter. I've got tons of homework but feel it's important that I "talk" with you tonight. So, here goes, although Ema would kill me if she knew I was writing you.

We talked about the peace discussions in Dayton and the bombings at dinner. Mr. Barnes said he thought there was a good chance the war would end soon. Almost before he was finished, Ema said that she was going to make plans to go home as soon as that happened. Mr. Barnes asked if she'd leave before the school year was finished, and she said yes, and asked if there was something wrong with that. He said he thought she should consider completing the school year and asked me if I planned to leave too.

I said I didn't know, that I wanted to see you so badly, but also wanted to see what college in America would be like. My BIG mistake was saying there's nothing to go home to, and Ema went ballistic. She asked what about you, Dzukela, and our friends and called me a traitor.

I tried to tell her that even you say Sarajevo is in shambles. Here we have hope and opportunities and will be free to choose what we do, while in Sarajevo, there will be nothing to choose.

Ema asked what could be more important than being with our family? Being in our own country?

I thought Mr. Barnes would calm her down when he told her that there was no right or wrong, that I had some difficult and important decisions to make about my education.

But Ema said he had no idea what it was really like at home, that he only knows what he reads in the newspapers or sees on TV, that he lives in a country that worries more about O.J. Simpson than ethnic cleansing.

Mr. Barnes said Ema was right, that he only knows what he reads, but he does know the importance of an education, and if I get into Princeton, it will be difficult for me to turn down an opportunity like that. He called it a complicated issue.

Ema said there is no issue, that family and country must come first.

Now that I've written this, I'm not sure why I did. Maybe to let off a little steam or prepare you for what might happen if the war ends.

Or simply because I needed to connect with you in some way because I miss you so much. I hope this helps us both.
Your devoted Irma

When she's finished reading, Sandra wonders how Jusuf would have reacted to the letter. Was Irma going to college in America and perhaps never returning to Bosnia upsetting to him, or would he think it was an inevitable outcome of the course he'd charted for her? And would he be proud of Ema and her loyalty to family and Bosnia? She thinks the answer to that question is definitely "yes."

∞

IN MID-DECEMBER, Sandra sets two glasses filled with Slivovitz—one for her and one for her beloved Jusuf—by the radio to celebrate the official announcement of the long-hoped-for peace. Their favorite broadcaster, her voice trembling with excitement, wastes no time in getting to the featured story:

The most prolonged city siege in the history of modern warfare is over! December 14, 1995, is a day to be celebrated. It will be remembered as one of the most important and joyous days in our country's history. In Paris, within the past hour, representatives from Croatia, the Federal Republic of Yugoslavia, and Bosnia and Herzegovina ratified the Dayton Accords' final version that divides Bosnia Herzegovina into two entities: Republika Srpska and the Federation of Bosnia and Herzegovina. What's more, there is already talk of trying Slobodan Milosevic and Radovan Karadzic for genocide and crimes against humanity by the International Criminal Tribunal in the Hague.

History will show that our war—and it was ours alone for over three devastating years—lasted three times as long as the Battle of Stalingrad and a year longer than the siege of Leningrad. But now it's finally over.

Finally.

Over.

On this 1,347th day, this last day of the siege, 5,434 Sarajevan civilians have been reported killed or missing, bringing the total number of civilian deaths in Bosnia to almost 40,000. And, lest we forget them, 166 UN soldiers have been killed trying to make us all safer. On the positive side, 1.8 million Bosnian refugees can return to their homes. In addition, NATO will deploy 60,000 troops as part of Operation Joint Endeavor to enforce the Accords and help keep the peace here at home. So until tomorrow, this is Lana Ulak for Radio Sarajevo 202, urging you to count your blessings and find a little joy in your life. You've earned it. We've all earned it.

Sandra taps one of the glasses against the other, raises it toward the radio, and says, "Here's to Jusuf, and here's to peace." Then, with tears flowing freely down her cheeks, she smiles and says, "Down the hatch," and empties each glass.

THAT EVENING as she begins to prepare her dinner, a heavy pounding resonates through the empty house. When Sandra opens the door, Milan reaches for her. She pulls away, and Milan grabs the door jamb to keep from falling. "Good Lord, Milan, have you been drinking?"

He doesn't answer. He simply stares at her, then clumsily tries to brush past her to enter the house.

Sandra raises a hand and says, "No, Milan, it's over, so go away. Please, go away and let me alone."

Milan lurches toward her again. "I'm not here to hurt you; I've come to apologize."

"To me? For what?"

"No. Not to you. To the Professor. He tried to be a good friend, and I didn't, and I'm sorry. He was a better man than I am."

Sandra stares at Milan. A Serb like her. A man who once again would want to be Jusuf's friend. The thought of Jusuf causes her to tear. She thinks of his modest demeanor, his devotion to his family and his music, his shyness when they first made love. She treasures his devotion to her and tries to imagine what he would do if he were still alive. She hesitates and then reaches for Milan's hand and says, "I have some coffee. You need to sober up a bit before you head on home."

2014

EMA WAITS PATIENTLY outside the heavy double door to Sandra's new house on Logavina Street. Thin and stylishly dressed, she is smiling, for she has brought her adopted grandmother a surprise; a café latte and her favorite pastry, a custard-filled krofne from Café Tito.

Sandra welcomes her with a long embrace and urges her to come in quickly and get settled. "I'm waiting to hear the news about the concert tonight."

They sit, their knees pressed against each other's, and Sandra tunes in Radio Sarajevo 202. "Let's listen to what Lana has to say."

Ema giggles. "She's Lana, now, is she? Like she's a member of the family?"

"In a way, she is. I've been listening to her for over twenty years. Your Dedo and I tried to hear her as often as we could."

Ema kisses her on the cheek. "Got it, Baka. I understand completely. It makes me happy, too, kind of like he's still with us, that his heart didn't fail him. But . . ."

"But what?" Sandra asks.

"I wish Irma was with us. Tonight would make her so proud."

"I'm sure it would, but she seems so happy in America," Sandra says and presses a finger to her lips as the reporter begins her morning report.

The World Health Organization has identified the spread of wild poliovirus as a public health emergency of international concern. They recommend implementing intensified eradication strategies in Cameroon, Equatorial Guinea, Pakistan, and the Syrian Arab Republic, saying that the worldwide spread of poliovirus threatens global efforts to eradicate one of the world's most serious vaccine-preventable diseases.

In Nigeria, it's reported that the jihadist terrorist organization, Boko Haram, has massacred 310 people. The attack, which lasted over twelve hours, began in a crowded market open at night so shoppers could escape the brutal daytime temperatures. Eventually, the rampage spread to the burning of many homes and the shooting of their residents. In what has become Boko Haram's trademark, several young teenage girls were abducted by the terrorists. The situation strikes an all too familiar chord and is a little too close to home for this reporter. Does it never end?

But here's some uplifting news. Tonight, the completion of the fourteen-year, 50-million-euro restoration of our Vijecnica will be celebrated by an event in Bascarsija Square that features the Sarajevo Philharmonic. Vedran Smailovic, the now-famous "Cellist of Sarajevo," will be the featured soloist. It promises to be a wonderful evening of entertainment, and I hope to see many of you there.

The reporter pauses for an uncomfortable moment, causing Ema and Sandra to exchange puzzled looks.

Now, if I can get through my goodbyes, here goes. Today, May 10, 2014, The Accords are still holding, tenuously perhaps, but still holding. And this old lady is signing off for the last time, with optimism for our futures but with sadness for leaving you, my many supportive listeners. As always, this is Lana Ulak for Radio Sarajevo 202, urging you never to forget what we have experienced and be careful and safe. And, please, for heaven's sake, find a little joy in your life.

A THANK YOU NOTE

There are four people who, without their loving guidance, these novellas would never have seen the light of day.

The first are Hattie and Rudi Laveran, who patiently chronicled the process and the pain of treating advanced colorectal cancer. In "Giant of the Valley," Big Louis' second daughter, Julia, is modeled after Hattie, who is a survivor of that life-threatening condition and merciless treatment. And Rudi provided a physician's perspective while facing many of the struggles of Julia's husband.

The idea to write "The Witness" came from a trip that Lyn and I took to Sarajevo in 1991. As a consultant to The Community of Bosnia, Lyn counseled many teenage Bosnian refugees who had fled for foster homes in the US. Her mission in Bosnia was to encourage local companies and NGOs to entice these talented young people back home.

Over the thirty years since our trip, I wrote several iterations of this story until I settled on telling it through the eyes of an elderly witness. Azra Hromadžić and Dženita Saračević, who both left Bosnia during the war or shortly thereafter, led me step by step through Sarajevo during the siege. There is no way I can thank them adequately for sharing their experiences and knowledge. They were of immeasurable value.

In addition to these four principal advisors, thanks go to Helen Cunningham for opening her home to Azra for five years when she moved to America. Helen's loving understanding of these young Bosnian women and their trials and tribulations of moving to a foreign land is the basis for Jusuf's granddaughters' experience in their new home.

Once again, I'm indebted to Anne Dubuisson, whose editorial insights energize me and make my stories better, and Franklyn "Buck" Rodgers, a steadfast reader and cheerleader.

As always, thanks to Lyn, whose insights make my stories and my life better and more interesting.

Author photo © Georgia Groome

ABOUT THE AUTHOR

Harry Groome is the former chairman of SmithKline Beecham Consumer HealthCare and a Governor Emeritus of The Nature Conservancy. He is the author of four novels: *Wing Walking*, *Thirty Below*, *Celebrity Cast*, and *The Best of Families* (the winner of the Indie Reader Discovery Award for Popular Fiction), along with the Stieg Larsson parody "The Girl Who Fished with a Worm." His short stories, poems, and articles have appeared in dozens of magazines and anthologies. Harry and his wife Lyn divide their time between Villanova, Pennsylvania, and the Adirondack Mountains in New York.

Visit Harry's website at www.harrygroome.com

Made in the USA
Middletown, DE
27 July 2022

70095444R00142